THE
HERD

When Democracy Falls

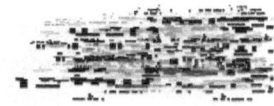

THE HERD

BOOK 1

**A POST-APOCALYPTIC DYSTOPIAN THRILLER
OF INFORMATION WARS AND LOVE**

ISBN: 979-8-9988323-0-7

This is a work of fiction. Names, characters, places, incidents, and dialogues are either products of the author's imagination or are used fictitiously. Any resemblance to actual persons, living or dead, events, or locales is entirely coincidental.

This edition is published by Jam Global Strategies LLC.

For more information, visit: www.jennyabamu.com

Cover design by 99Designs
Interior design by Jenny Abamu

Printed in the United States of America.

Visit my website and join the mailing list.
www.jennyabamu.com

Disclaimer

This is a work of fiction. While the story and characters are products of the author's imagination, the book explores themes of police violence, murder, assault, and other difficult subjects. It also contains sexual content and explicit language, which may be triggering for some readers. The author has approached these topics with care and respect, aiming to shed light on complex human experiences. Reader discretion is advised. If you or someone you know is affected by similar issues, please seek support from a trusted professional or helpline.

For my husband, Sedat, who stuck with me through the creation of this art.

PART ONE
THE TEST

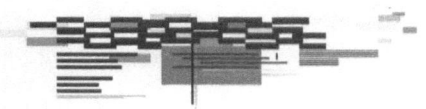

1

Washington, D.C., 2065

I slide the story toward the editor and wait for a response. He curses while furiously striking his keyboard.

"Fucking idiot, these fools will believe anything." He doesn't look up or reach for the paper. "Is this what the bots gave you?"

"I—" I pause, unsure if I should tell him the truth. "I made some changes. I had to—"

"Again?" He finally looks at me.

I wipe my sweaty palms against my jeans and calculate my words.

"The numbers were off. I ran it several times on my own. Changes the whole story," I manage to choke out the truth.

The fury from his fingers engulfs his hand like flames as he slams his fist against the desk. His mouse and keypad jump, and the precious coffee others in the outside world would literally kill each other to have spills on the ground.

"Damn it." His eyes dart toward the coffee.

He stands up and trudges towards me. Instinctively, I stumble backwards and graze my hands over the dagger hidden on my waist.

He keeps marching toward me, and I keep backing away until I hit his cold mahogany door. I keep my eyes on him while feeling for the handle, wishing I had left it open. I inhale and exhale with each step he takes.

"You will not tell anyone about this," he says, digging his finger into my shoulder and fogging my glasses with his breath.

"We are working on an update, and there are a few kinks. We don't want anyone to needlessly panic. You understand?"

I nod slowly.

"Very well then." He takes a few steps back, leans against his desk, and lets out a deep breath.

"Thank you again for making the corrections. It's imperative that we have and maintain trust. You are dismissed."

Relieved, I whip around, open the door, and bolt out of the room. But just as I am turning the corner, I catch a glimpse of the stack of papers I left on his desk hanging over the trash bin.

That was three months ago.

***

My sweaty hands grip the edge of my desk as I sit at my usual workspace, waiting for my name to be called. I close my eyes and try to tune out the noisy beeps and churns of the machines and chatter all around me. I've waited four years for this moment, but somehow I still don't feel ready.

I work as a contractor for one of the largest news networks in the world, the only network on this side of the Atlantic to survive the crash and resist acquisition by either a billionaire or the government. People tell me I'm lucky to be here, that many desire my job, and so I should be happy. And I am happy, or at least I think I am.

I work in the heart of the news station, which buzzes like a factory. There are about ten long tables in parallel rows, each with about ten editors seated next to machines that resemble printers but possess the artificial intelligence of advanced bots. These machines scan the internet, smart devices, and all types of digital outputs for announcements and credible leads for news stories, then assemble the first drafts of stories for the editors to review. The editors review the drafts, make the necessary changes, and upload the articles. But most of the time, they simply upload the drafts since the machines have become so advanced that they hardly need editing. Once the higher-ups in the station approve the stories, they are published, and the editors share them on social media. I sit in the third seat on the first row.

Our seating is a sign of rank. Editors say it can take years to get to the first row, but I did it just after two.

I stare at the paper the bot has spewed out for me to review. It's about the poverty rate throughout the country. According to the raw copy, based on leaked government records, the numbers have remained stable for the last six months. My fingers glide across the bot's screen, requesting the dataset the computer has used. With a quick glance, I notice several errors.

Another one, I think to myself. *That's the fourth time this week!*

Lately, I've been catching a lot of these mistakes. It started about five months ago when I was bored and picked up one of the rare history books my uncle left me about what used to be the United States economy before the crash. While reading, I noticed a historical detail in the book that directly contradicted something I saw in one of the bot stories I edited and published earlier that day. As I dug deeper into the details and reviewed the story, I found multiple inaccuracies.

Since then, I've gone down rabbit holes with these bot stories, checking and double-checking. Normally, I try to keep a low profile, but there were so many mistakes I decided to alert some senior editors. They supposedly looked into it and told me it's nothing but an update bug. I don't know if I believe them. Something feels off.

I also have a strange feeling I've been watched more closely since reporting the incident. People know who I am, but for years I've successfully laid low. My father had a reputation for constantly shaking things up, and I saw firsthand what it cost him and my family.

Truth is, there's not much value in shaking things up these days. We need the station. People need something they can trust. I need something I can trust.

My mind returns to the story. It's clear from the data that certain regions have been severely undercounted. I decide to rework the headline and the story. It now reads, "Bogus Numbers Keep the True National Poverty Rate Hidden."

I stare at the bot next to me, wondering if I need to report this uptick in errors again—not just from what the bots spew out but also from what I see published. It worries me that the public might begin to question our credibility. But I also wonder, who am I to bring up such accusations?

"Feonix, Feonix!" A voice jolts me from my thoughts.

I look up to see Emre hovering over my desk. I tense, instinctively wary of his intentions.

"Uhhh, hi," I reply, confused, wondering why after all this time he has decided to make conversation today.

His hazel eyes meet my brown ones as I look up. He's tall and handsome, with a mischievous grin that makes me wonder if he knows something I don't. The way he carries himself, people might assume he thinks he's better than everyone else—present but a bit aloof, as if he has better things to do than this job. I assume he's talking to me because of the competition and nothing more. But as his eyes pierce mine, I almost hold my breath, waiting for his reply. I'm not trying to get caught up in any more station entanglements, but I cannot deny that Emre has swag.

"I know we haven't spoken much," he says slowly, seeming unsure of what to say next, "but I wanted to say good luck tomorrow—not that you need it. You make this look easy."

There's a sincerity in his voice that catches me off guard, as if he genuinely cares about my fate. It makes me want to believe that perhaps not everyone here is part of the facade. Maybe, just maybe, I could afford to let my guard down. But old habits die hard.

"We haven't spoken at all," I snap back at him, immediately regretting the harshness of my words. "And I really don't have the time to start today."

His half-smile fades to a frown, and for a second, I want to kick myself for being a bitch again. I could maybe use a friend, or at least one less enemy in this process. But my instincts remain, and instead of apologizing, I give him a look that says, "Why are you still here?"

His beautiful eyes dim as his pleasant demeanor vanishes. He walks back to his seat in the second row. If my response has dejected him, he doesn't show it as he quickly resumes his work. I can't help but notice how he nervously taps his fingers on the table, something I've seen him do when he's deep in thought. I wonder what he's thinking about now. Probably that I'm such a bitch.

I shake my head as if to clear it and look back down at my computer. My hands shake, and my face feels flushed. I suddenly thank my lucky stars for the melanin in my skin.

Get it together, I think to myself. *What an outsized reaction to a basic greeting.*

The bot lights up. My story has been approved. The tension in my body drains away with this realization, then immediately tenses again as I remember what else I have to do. I've come to enjoy most of my work, but sharing on social media always gives me anxiety. Some editors are obsessed, arguing with every bot and person online. They thrive on the drama, the relentless back-and-forth exchanges that give them a sense of purpose. And somehow, all the belligerence and hot takes have garnered them large followings. To me, social media interactions have always seemed disingenuous. We all know we put up a facade there. Would they say that shit to my face? I know they wouldn't.

Up until two years ago, my account looked like a bot's. I followed a few people, like the news director (everyone follows the news director), and only a few people from my neighborhood followed me. But two years ago, I decided I needed to do more to qualify for the Aptitude Test. Now, I have thousands of followers.

There's only one news director position, and for years, they have been looking for a successor. To narrow the choice down fairly, years ago, the station director announced that the person with the highest score on the Aptitude Test, when she either passes the baton because she can no longer work or passes away, will be the successor.

But to even qualify for the test, you must be a Station 7 employee and have at least 300,000 social followers—the concept being that you must be both intelligent and exhibit leadership. Few contractors qualify, and none have passed any part of the test. So I certainly stand out, and I know it.

But today is my last day as an editor because my contract is about to expire, and—in order to fulfill my promise to my uncle—I decide to take the Aptitude Test. I will probably fail. I am not a leader. I don't even have friends. But I made a promise.

If I pass the test with the highest score, I'll take over this building as the head of the source of information that has given me and others hope for so many years—an improbable scenario.

If I lose, the more likely outcome, I don't really have a next step planned. There's not much planning that can be done with life outside of the station, only trying to survive.

After all I've done, I have never been offered a full-time role. I guess I'm not perky or likable enough. I applied so many times but am always told they feel a different candidate is a better fit. Maybe it's all my complaints about the bots. Either way, my time as an editor expires because my contract will be up, and I'll have nowhere to go.

I've known for a while that my time was ticking, so two years ago, I amped up my social strategy to qualify. Station 7 employees often get more followers than most people because of the organization's reputation. Two years ago, I had 6,804 followers. But when I started taking the work more seriously—spotting mistakes the bots made, staying up late to take on challenging stories, and not only sharing my stories but also the process behind them—my following exploded. Now I have about 450,000 people following every post I make, giving me many more followers than I need to qualify.

"This will be one of my last story explanations," I begin typing my next post to my followers.

"I've entered the contest. I will start the Aptitude Test tomorrow," I continue.

"If I win, I hope I can be half the leader Director Revel is, consistently upholding the truth.

Thank you all for your support. I hope you will continue to follow and support me."

I hesitate for a minute, reading the message about three times. Then I hit send.

Immediately, my screen lights up with notifications, and my following grows by the thousands. Every time someone enters the Aptitude Test, they gain thousands of followers. Though the details of the test are secret, people update their followers as they pass certain parts, and followers root for contestants like sports teams.

I wonder who these followers are. I wonder how many of them root for me to succeed. Then I consider how many of them want me to fail.

I close the screen and take a deep breath. I try to hide my anxiety, which has built to mountainous proportions by this time. It's coming from not only from the fact that I am taking the test but also because I waited until the last minute to do it.

I close my eyes.

"Idiot, you are an idiot," my father's words echo in my ear.

"Where will you go when you fail?" I imagine him questioning me. "Once you lose, you'll be thrown to the wolves. Chicken shit. You have a month, then you'll be back in the streets with the rest of the trash where you belong."

2

What Happens After Trust Collapses?

Beep, beep, beep. Notifications from my phone snap me out of my haze.

I take a deep breath and stand. I need air and a stroke of good luck. I figure if I leave for a short time, I won't miss my name being called. I head to the locker room to change.

When I enter, a group of young women laughing loudly suddenly drops their voices to whispers and observe me from the corner of their eyes.

"Good luck, Feonix," says Stacey.

Stacey is tall, smart, beautiful, curvy, with silky brown hair and perfectly dewy skin—so many things I am not. I try not to resent her for just existing the way she does.

"T-thanks," I reply, hesitant.

These interactions are always a bit awkward because, when it's time for the test, people truly don't know if they will ever see you again. I take off my uniform and glance at my athletic frame, wishing I had a bit more of the curves Stacey does.

Then I slip on my worn, patched-up leather jacket, threadbare jeans, and battered sneakers.

Stacey looks like she wants to say more—maybe "bye forever." But I don't wait for the awkwardness to linger. I grab my things and head toward the building's garage. There, I check out the most battered Station 7 vehicle and drive out.

Beyond the station—a rare occurrence given the chaos outside—I make sure to drive inconspicuously. I try to blend in, appearing as worn and beaten as possible to avoid attracting the attention of robbers or gang members prowling the streets.

It's been 23 tumultuous years since a sinister collaboration between China and Russia unleashed an information war that toppled the U.S. economy, snatched jobs away, ignited riots, and coerced Americans into joining factions. Whispers of underground information wars circulated for years—pro-Black activists' social media pages run by Russians, and American-appearing white supremacy blogs churned out by the Chinese. But when the war erupted, barraging the public with a relentless stream of messaging online, on the radio, on television, through smart speakers, and in text messages, no one was prepared—especially not the government.

Elected officials became the primary purveyors of disinformation, spreading outright lies in a desperate bid for votes from a disenfranchised, distrustful, and despondent public.

I drive past the haunting remnants of a once-magnificent bank building in one of Washington, D.C.'s wealthiest neighborhoods. Bloodstained ropes still dangle from its sides—a chilling memorial to the public hanging of bankers, investors, and any other affluent-looking person the furious mob of years past could seize after the crash.

Russia and China targeted the economy with laser-like precision, disseminating fear-mongering information to stock market investors, bitcoin bros, and every other kind of dealer you could think of, goading them into a frenzied selling spree that sent market valuations into a nosedive.

Countless people lost everything. As faith in the government withered, they took it upon themselves to administer their own brutal brand of justice.

Suddenly, I feel the car shudder. Someone tries to pry open the back door and clamber inside. The other back door starts shaking too.

"Damn it, gangs," I mutter, my heart racing.

Normally, I'd be ready for this kind of assault, but today, my mind is swathed in a fog of anxiety about the Aptitude Test.

My foot slips for a moment as I try to switch from the brake to the gas. Just as I hear the shattering of one of my car windows, my foot slams onto the gas pedal, and I speed away from the assailants.

A rock wrapped in newspaper crashes through the passenger window. Cold air nips at my cheek, but I can't help wondering where they found the newspaper.

Before the crash, the independent American news media was already fragile, reeling from the loss of advertising dollars to social networks and celebrities who often boasted more followers than the most popular news outlets. The crash dealt the final, crushing blow.

Initially, networks struggled to counter the flood of propaganda from all directions. As they attempted to debunk lies and remind audiences that stories cited by congressmen or excerpts in the president's speeches were sourced from falsehoods, these sources only gained more traction.

Disinformation had been festering on society's fringes for years. Outlandish conspiracy theories found a home among small groups of neglected and disenfranchised people. The more these theories spread, the more people subconsciously grew accustomed to them—until even those who wouldn't normally entertain such ideas began to consciously embrace them.

Overseas information warmongers targeted the free media, casting doubt on their work by distorting reporters' words, exploiting private chats, and highlighting mistakes to claim bias. Their goal was to discredit, and they succeeded.

Before everything went haywire, newsrooms had cut funding for editors and fact-checkers while ramping up production. Reporters churned out stories at breakneck speed, sacrificing accuracy to meet demand.

So when foreign actors unleashed their information war on the U.S. news media, public trust crumbled. Then, when the economic crash struck, fragile U.S. news groups were wiped out—losing venture capital funding and public support, laying off thousands.

For a brief period, it seemed like all independent news media had vanished, leaving only billionaires and government agencies to spew messages through every available channel.

Without independent media as a check, American government-run news agencies devolved into propaganda tools. President Michael Dickson declared a state of emergency and incessantly broadcast his messages. He implemented desperate economic policies, slashing interest rates and offering funding to the poor, but these measures did little to alleviate the harsh realities people faced.

Inflation soared. Those on minimum wages—about 40 percent of the employed population—could no longer afford basic goods like bread, eggs, and milk. People formed gangs, raiding grocery stores. Protests escalated into nationwide riots. America, once a pillar of democracy, crumbled.

Before long, the riots reached the White House. To the horror of democratic societies worldwide, President Dickson's administration ended with a mob hanging, streamed live across multiple platforms.

The new president, former mob leader Jeffrey Lewis, clamped down even harder on all media outlets. He transformed the FBI and the Department of Homeland Security into a police force that monitored traditional and social media for "terroristic ideas." Overnight, people found to harbor such ideas were arrested and thrown into makeshift prisons. The waiting times for court hearings stretched into years. With Senate support, he suspended constitutional rights, claiming he needed to control the messaging to stabilize the economy and rebuild the country. If people disagreed, their dissent was considered a threat to national stabilization, and they were also labeled terrorists.

All billionaire-owned news entities existed solely to amass profit for the wealthiest Americans, safeguard their interests, and provide them with exclusive information while distorting facts to manipulate the public and squeeze out more profits. Most wealthy Americans retreated into gated parts of cities, isolating themselves from the struggling masses. Reporters at billionaire-run news agencies, largely replaced by printer-bots, focused only on gathering business intelligence to sell at exorbitant prices. Consequently, the majority of the population was left in the dark and economically disadvantaged.

The fourth estate, once meant to bring checks and balances to power, was effectively shattered for several years. Governments and billionaires, both domestic and foreign, waged relentless information wars against each other and the people they governed. The rich grew richer as the middle class plummeted into poverty. The powerful monopolized information to maintain their grip on power, even at the nation's expense.

Amidst the chaos, Station 7, my workplace, emerged from the rubble. Initially, a small group of renegade engineers ran the operation, releasing short articles auto-generated through algorithmic code. This sent government officials into a frenzy as they tried to locate and apprehend them.

The code incorporates popular news-writing principles like varied introductions and putting the most engaging information at the top of a story. The articles are based on information sourced from scanners that scour the internet, with source code free from Russian or Chinese influence.

Station 7 employed a single human editor to review the information before it went online. This editor quickly gained a devoted following for producing and fearlessly revealing information no government or billionaire-owned news agency will touch. She became a beacon of hope for many across the nation and the world, her image synonymous with truth, bravery, and resistance in a world that had forsaken democratic ideals.

Now, she is the news director, answerable only to the public that donates what little they can to keep the network afloat.

Station 7 evolved from a covert operation to a public one. Its headquarters blossomed from the ground like a flower in the desert. Though the director remained a wanted figure, her popularity grew so immense that an army of supporters rose to defend the building every time government forces approached. For them, keeping Station 7 alive and thriving is a cause worth dying for.

I finally arrive at my old apartment building. I park the car in an alleyway, hoping it won't draw unwanted attention. Then I enter the half-empty structure. With my hand on the knife strapped to my hip, I wonder why I even came back. The polluted soot in the air reminds me that I couldn't even get the breath of fresh air I was hoping for.

Although I know many of the apartments in this building are vacant, I feel eyes on me as I sprint through the hallways and navigate corners searching for my old apartment.

This will likely be one of my last visits, I think.

I eventually find it—the door to our old apartment. The wood shows beneath the chipped gray paint. I push on the door, and to my surprise, it opens with a small creak. I cautiously step inside, scanning each corner for potential threats. Memories flood back.

As a teenager, I remember sketching the station director's image onto a piece of scrap paper. Her fiery red hair billows in the wind, her intense green eyes stare back at me from the paper. My uncle adored it so much that he hung it on the door.
"This could be you one day," he used to tell me. "We must never lose hope, or we'll become the savages all around us."

I nodded to appease him, but deep down, I never believed it. I could hardly fathom finding food for the next day, let alone running a place like Station 7. It was clear my uncle saw something in me that I couldn't see in myself.

Six years ago, the news director sent shockwaves across the globe when she announced that she was suffering from an incurable disease that would ultimately claim her life. She sought a successor for the station, someone she planned to mentor until her final breath.

That night, my uncle and I embraced each other, tears streaming down our faces. Despite having only a few candles to ration for light, we attended a vigil outside Station 7, using our limited wick to honor her. It felt as though a beloved family member had fallen ill.

Her impending death inspired those with sinister ambitions, and that year, violence escalated.

No accurate count could be confirmed since the government didn't maintain reliable records.

About a year after the announcement, my uncle staggered into our shabby one-bedroom apartment, clutching his side. A stab wound oozed blood.

"They took everything I had," he mumbles, choking on the blood bubbling in his throat.

My memories of that moment are fragmented. I recall screaming, desperately trying to stop the bleeding with a blanket, and the look of despair in his eyes. He wasn't afraid of death, but he dreaded leaving me alone in this cruel world. As I held him and sobbed, he made me promise to pursue the news director position. I sat with his lifeless body in my arms until it grew cold and still.

The next day, I buried him in a lot behind our building. Though I doubted God's existence, I prayed for my uncle's eternal peace.

Later that afternoon, I spotted a man in the distance wearing my uncle's jacket. Rage consumed me as I realized he must be the one who robbed and killed my uncle. I charged toward him without any regard for my own safety.

I must have caught him off guard because, in no time, he was on the ground, and I was punching without control—hoping to pummel his face deeper and deeper into the cement until I could feel the rocks on the other side of his head. After a few hits, I pulled out my dagger and prepared to gut him like a fish.

He screamed, begging for his life, offering my uncle's jacket and wallet. I suddenly felt the deep pain of my uncle's loss, and my eyes began to swell with tears. But I refused to let that monster witness my grief. I took the wallet and jacket and raced home.

Aware that only station employees can vie for the news director position, I cleaned myself with a rag, changed clothes, and headed to apply for an opening at the station that same day.

Walking around the apartment, I notice the bookshelf still leaning against the wall. I can see the initials my uncle and I etched into it one night when I couldn't find him after waking from a nightmare. He was out bartering for money at the time, and when he came home and saw me terrified and sobbing, he reassured me that if he was ever absent, I could simply place my hand on those initials to feel his presence and dispel my loneliness.

Tears well up in my eyes as I trace the carved letters.

"I really need you now," I think.

It's as if my uncle is there to warn me; I sense danger approaching. Instinctively, I drop low and prepare to flee. I hear three men enter the room.

"You sure she came in here?" one man questions.

"Positive," another voice confirms.

"Hey, pretty thing, we won't hurt you too bad," taunts a third voice. "It'll be quick and painless if you enjoy it."

My mind races. Three against one—bastards.

Then, suddenly, as if my uncle is still there guiding me, I spot the fire extinguisher. It appears to be in working condition. I stand up and yank the extinguisher off the wall. Startled, the men charge toward me. I pull the lever, unleashing a spray that clouds our vision, but I've already mapped my escape route. I hurl the extinguisher at one attacker's head and sprint for the door.

As I reach the threshold, one man lunges, grasping my heel, and we both tumble to the floor. Adrenaline surges through me.

"Get the hell off me, you bastard!"

He clamps down harder with his other hand, smirking. Rage consumes me as I think of all the women and young girls they must have tormented over the years. Without hesitation, I whip out my knife and plunge it into both his wrists.

His smile morphs from shock to agony in slow motion as he registers what just transpired. I break free and sprint for the car, driving straight back to the station.

"Fucking fresh air," I mutter, shaking my head at that stupidly unnecessary adventure.

When I get back to the station, I sit in my seat, exhausted and bloodied.

"Feonix Cheenoma," the sound of my name through my headphones snaps me out of my thoughts.

"Group B, contestant 3," announces the robotic voice.

I hastily jot down the number and group letter on a sheet of paper, curious about the others in my group. I shake off the worry, knowing I'll find out tomorrow. I resume my work—only two hours left as an editor.

***

At the end of the day, I gather all my things, aware that tomorrow morning someone else will take my place.

Like most Station 7 employees, my home is in the living quarters underground. I think about my apartment outside of the station. I remember my family.

Both of my parents and my little sister were killed when an angry mob attacked our faction's living quarters nine years ago. I was told that hysteria started to rise after the Russians pushed out an onslaught of propaganda reports against key leaders in our faction, alleging that they were working with the Chinese to embezzle government funds meant to go to the Patriots.

The Patriots faction is mostly made up of those who believe in extreme American nationalism. There had always been people who subscribed to some forms of nationalism. Before the fall, sayings like "America first" had become more pronounced.

But the economic crash—and the knowledge and fear that foreign actors were behind it—drew a new kind of fever out of people. The country split into factions that acted more like tribes. The most extreme people took over, drawing on the worst parts of their ideologies.

More than most factions, the Patriots suffered severe economic loss because of their refusal to trade goods with non-American entities. But for many of them, it was easier to believe that the source of their suffering is an outside faction that stressed tolerance for foreigners than to accept that their ideology is in conflict with their own economic well-being.

Patriot members quickly turned their anger and the pain of their economic loss toward innocent people within our faction, and one night, the group attacked us. Stores were robbed, and many homes were burned to the ground, including ours. I don't know who saved me from my burning apartment that day. I only remember the sooty building crumbling beneath my feet as the fire tore through the foundation.

I woke up in a hospital bed, terrified.

"Relax, little one," a nurse cupped my hands in hers.

I pulled away.

"Where am I? Where is my family?"

"They are gone, but you are safe now," she replied, her tightly curled hair pulled back in a bun.

The nurse told me I was lucky to be alive. My father, a newspaper reporter before the crash, had become the faction leader at the time we were attacked, and they intended to kill our entire family. I remember not comprehending all her words and wondering why anyone would want to kill my family.

I also didn't quite understand what she meant by "they are gone," because after that moment a part of me still expected to see them. But when I saw the sadness in her dark eyes, my own emotions—fear, sadness, and confusion—overwhelmed me, and I joined the weeping voices of many others who lost loved ones in the hospital.

After the incident, my uncle took me in. He was a quiet man, a historian and writer before the crash. Somehow, he managed to save several books that filled his tiny apartment, which felt more like living in a closet. He was still a reader and writer, though he sold used goods on the side of the road.

I spent my days reading many of the books in his apartment and digging through trash to help him find things to sell so we could survive. I also maintained an irrational fear that the people who killed my family will come back for me. I began training to protect myself with a knife I found and polished while rummaging through the trash one day.

In the evenings before bed, he talked for hours about "how things used to be." He always said he felt "overwhelmed" with the ignorance around him. He had a hard time watching people behave as if this is the way the United States has always been.

"How could they forget their own history so quickly?" he scoffed while watching a fight outside the window. "Savages."

Most days he seemed to waver between crankiness and loneliness. He lost his wife and son the night the Patriots attacked our faction. His only delight seemed to be in teaching me. He said teaching me made him feel like he had a purpose again, like he's doing his own little part "to save the next generation."

Where my dad tore me down, my uncle built me up. He taught me about the history behind our current state of affairs, who ran the news groups, what information could be trusted and what couldn't.

"Leader of the communist party during the Vietnam War," he quizzed.

"Ho Chi Minh," I replied.

"Theory that suggests that countries should specialize in the production of goods and services in which they have a lower opportunity cost and trade with other countr—," he continued.

"Theory of Comparative Advantage. David Ricardo. Early 19th century. Too easy," I smirked.

"No, you're too smart," my uncle looked at me as if in wonder.

"I'm not smart," I looked at the ground, shaking my head.

"Stop saying that. You're brilliant. You are a born leader. I loved your father, but he was a fool for not seeing that in you," he put his hand on my shoulder and closed the book.

I choked back the tears. My uncle pulled me close for a hug.

"There are so many things I wish Fred had done differently," he said. "But even the best heroes are flawed."

My uncle and I talked about almost everything, but he always has trouble talking about the night of the attack.

"It was like your dad knew something was coming," my uncle told me. "He knew something he never told me. A month before the attack, he had the same look he got when he stumbled onto something interesting. I wish he told me. Maybe we could have saved some people that night."

I could tell this mystery ate at him. Sometimes it ate at me too. I wanted to know what my dad knew. I wanted a more satisfying explanation for my family's death. Was it really just ignorance that drove the Patriots to attack?

It's this mystery that kept me from seeking revenge by killing Patriots like some in my faction chose to do after the attack.

I am more interested in learning the truth. Something in the story isn't complete. It's like the systematic breakdown of trustworthy information hits me on every level. This breakdown robs me of peace. It keeps my family alive in my dreams, as if, even in death, they won't let me rest without the truth.

I knew finding that truth will bring me to the front lines of the information war and could possibly get me killed. But I didn't know where to start until the day my uncle died.

3

A Team Effort, Try Not to Die

I feel overwhelmed with emotions the next morning.

It feels as if I have just been there—in our old home—arguing with my sister, my mom breaking up the fight. My dad is even there, his eyes twinkling as he smiles at me while serving us dinner. Then that twinkle turns into a flame and engulfs us all.

I wake up in sweats. I haven't had such nightmares in years.

But there's no time to decompress or try to understand why the nightmares have returned. Today is test day.

I pull myself out of bed. Normally, I get up just in time to dress and leave, but today I decide to give myself more time. My room is a mess, as usual, but somehow I know my way through the chaos.

I stumble toward the small coffee machine in my room and turn it on. Coffee is a luxury. I never had it when I lived with my uncle. We simply couldn't afford it. But with my salary from the station, I can purchase coffee from the grocery store in the cafeteria. My salary doesn't make me rich, but given the rate of poverty outside the station, I feel as if I'm part of the upper class. Coffee solidifies that feeling. It's one of the many comforts you can easily get at the station store but not from other grocers outside.

I get dressed while waiting for the coffee to brew. Normally, the newsroom requires business casual clothing, which for me means black slacks, a T-shirt, and a blazer. But for the aptitude test, we're told to dress comfortably. I grab blue jeans and a T-shirt from my clean laundry pile on the ground. Then I put on a used leather jacket I bought a few years ago.

I decide to grab two knives from my collection—just in case. Knives have become something of a small obsession ever since my uncle died. I train with them almost daily and collect them, too. Apart from coffee and books, I spend a significant part of my salary on new knives. I have knives that can be disguised as cell phones, lipsticks, and other accessories. The holes in the dartboard on my wall are proof that my aim has improved significantly.

After grabbing my coffee, I sit in front of my computer and open it. I have 560,000 followers now.

"So it begins," I type and hit send. Then I close the computer and leave the room.

There are five groups of four people competing for one open position: Groups A, B, C, D, and E, each with its own set of contestants, marked one through four. I find a seat in the theater room underneath a sign that reads "Group B." I can feel the sweat tingling on the back of my neck, but I try to appear confident, reminding myself that I am prepared for this.

The people on my team are both my companions and my competition today. I remind myself to be friendly but not get too attached. Throughout my time as an editor, I haven't made much headway in the friends department. You need to be open and sociable to make friends. I am none of those things. Up to this point, I've needed an accurate understanding of history, a prudent and detailed understanding of sourcing, and clear, concise writing—not friends.

"Hi, my name is Feonix." I extend my hand toward one of the guys approaching my section.

"Yeah, I've heard of you," he responds, shaking my hand. "I heard no mistake makes it past you. I'm James Han."

I can't help but stare a little longer than I should at him. He's tall and incredibly handsome. His brown eyes seem to shimmer against the light as he looks into mine, and his smile is warm but shows no weakness. I haven't seen many Americans of East Asian descent since our faction was attacked by the Patriots.

Though Americans from several ethnic identities suffered that night, few suffered like people of East Asian descent. They were already under stricter government surveillance. They were imprisoned for the smallest crimes. But when the Patriots thought our faction was colluding with the Chinese, they killed any American that appeared to have Asian ancestry indiscriminately, questioning their loyalty to America.

"Where are the others?" he asks, pulling his hand away from mine and snapping me out of my stare.

"I'm not sure," I reply, slightly embarrassed by his unease. I can see the other groups gathering in their own respective corners around the room.

"This is no way to begin," says James, sounding agitated.

I already like his attitude. He seems commanding and confident, like someone who came to win.

"Sorry we're late," two young guys—clearly related, one fat and one skinny—join our group.

"I'm Titan," says the fat one, extending his hand first to me. His fade is flawless, like he just did it yesterday.

"And I'm Ray," says the skinny one, also extending his hand. His short dreads bobble up and down with his head.

"Oh wait, I know who you are," says Titan, looking at me. "I heard Fred Cheenoma's daughter worked here, but I never thought I'd meet you."

"You're Fred Cheenoma's daughter?" asks Ray. "Your dad's a legend—at least for those of us from Latus."

"Who's your dad?" asks James, staring at me curiously.

I hesitate. I don't usually talk about my family with strangers. Ever since my parents passed away, I hardly have people approach me to speak about my father. Titan and Ray are clearly brothers from Latus.

"Depends. Who are you?" Titan asks, clearly sizing James up—both as a greeting and something more.

"James Han." James extends his hand to Titan.

"Pleasure to make your acquaintance," Titan says, shaking James's hand and holding on a little too long.

"Who was her dad?" James pulls his hand away.

"Oh yeah," Titan continues, making me feel better about my awkward handshake with James moments earlier. "Only one of the greatest reporters turned faction leaders of this century," he says, cutting me off before I can respond. "While he was in charge, Latus was one of the wealthiest and most educated factions. Nothing like how they are now.

Rumor has it that all the faction leaders wanted to work with him, but he refused because of their corruption. My parents said that's why they killed him. What they couldn't get through negotiations, they took by force."

Titan's words hit me like a knife. These are rumors I've heard before, but they always make me uneasy. I open my mouth to try to respond, but I am interrupted again.

"Enough of the pleasantries, teams. It's time to gather around," says a woman with thick, curly, reddish-brown hair and bold blue eyes. Something about her look is beautiful and exotic—clearly mixed race. Her personality is instantly appealing, like she should be the host of a show. She stands on stage, gesturing to the space on the ground in front of her. I feel drawn to her as I walk closer.

As we are shepherded forward, I notice Emre in Group A watching me. He tries to look away as soon as I notice him, but realizing he already has my attention, he offers a slight smile that I do not return.

"For most of you, this will be your first and last time meeting the news director because only one of you will be chosen to eventually take her position," the woman on stage continues. "Remember, you must tell no one about the tests you are about to go through."

Something about the spectacle seems theatrical. The woman speaks as if she is putting on a show, like we are being watched on film for someone's entertainment. Though people are clearly nervous, her tone also seems to excite the contestants. They begin to whisper and squirm among themselves. For a second, it is almost as if we are entering a fun competition where our sole means of survival isn't at stake.

Then suddenly, the room falls silent as the news director appears in front of us for the first time. Her red hair is bright, shining under the lights on the stage. She seems to study us intently as she walks out, registering every face gazing up toward her.

"My name is Victoria Revel, and I am the news director here at Station 7," she says, taking the microphone from the other woman on stage. "I like to explain the rules of the tests myself because if you pass the Aptitude test with the highest score, your training to take over the newsroom will come from me. And if you can't listen to me now, you won't be a good protégé later."

"First, I want you all to know that regardless of whether or not you are chosen, you have done your part in this war. Our enemies are both cunning and well-resourced, putting us in a position where we need the best and brightest to run this operation," she pauses, looking around to meet eyes with at least one person from each group.

"It has been a combination of your courage, leadership, hard work, and intelligence that has brought you this far. Now, we must learn how far those qualities, in addition to other attributes, extend."

As she explains the rules for the first test, I slowly begin to realize that these tests are nothing like what I imagined. They drop us directly into the chaos of our real world, closer to the subjects our news covers than I have ever been.

"This could get us killed," blurts out one girl from Group A—Emre's group—after the instructions are given. I am relieved to hear that I am not the only person finding it hard to believe what we are being asked to do.

"If you are worried about your life, then you are not ready for war. This is an information war!" yells the news director back at the girl.

Revel's fists are balled, and she is shaking with rage. The girl seems to shrink under Revel's gaze, looking as if she is holding back tears. No one else says a word.

I feel my stomach turn as fear creeps up my spine. I have heard of multiple people from our news group dying in the course of gathering information for stories. Many of them are admired, seen as martyrs for a great cause. I admire them. But it never occurred to me that they may be in the middle of a test.

The newsroom received a tip that multiple faction representatives are accepting various forms of compensation from the Saudi government in exchange for spreading allegations that Iranian leaders are working to replace democratically elected leaders in various countries and to attack Americans. This is reportedly part of an effort to turn public sentiment in the United States and other parts of the world against Iran, so the Saudis can attack the Iranians without fear of rebuke.

For years, those two countries have been powerful forces in the Middle East. Their economies thrive on oil and natural gas resources that seem endless. For a time, some thought their power would diminish because of the global push toward renewable energy sources, like solar. But when the crash occurred, investments in renewable energy dried up, making the two countries stronger than ever. Since the U.S. maintained good relations with both countries, accepting their aid to rebuild, they are more powerful now than before.

World order shifted as countries saw the crash and the weakness of the United States as an opportunity to reject the status quo and redraw boundaries as they saw fit. To the terror of many in Europe, Russia started to rebuild something that resembled the former USSR, annexing Georgia, Ukraine, Finland, and Poland in bloody battles.

The Saudi Kingdom annexed all of the Gulf countries in its periphery—Bahrain, Yemen, Oman, and later the UAE and Qatar—with equal force. And now, it appears they are looking to take on their powerful regional foe, Iran. If they take over Iran, they will be the most powerful country in the region—maybe the world.

But most Americans are less concerned about the vast nature of the Saudis' plans. Their concerns are domestic issues. They would be horrified to learn their leaders are accepting money from foreign sources to deceive them—horrified enough to remove and hang the representatives.

So much has changed in the United States since the crash. Faction leaders are more like what senators used to be, but with less organization and more power. The crash caused an erosion of trust between the people, the federal government, and all its representatives. It led the American people to turn away from the existing system and begin to create their own.

Factions are part of the new order. Their leaders represent groups of people who share ideas without boundaries, meaning a faction leader can represent one person in Oregon and another in Texas. Though many people cluster with those who share their own ideology and faction.

Faction leaders gain voting power based on the number of people registered in their faction. There are many different groups: the communists, called Sumbolas; the nationalists, known as the Patriots; the religious Christians, called the Divinus; the capitalists, known as Opes; the socially liberal, known as Latus; and so on. There is even a faction for those who officially subscribe to no faction or ideology—Tantum—where I and many others in the newsroom currently belong.

But the factions share one thing in common—everything the people in them do is based on a collective sense of loyalty to the faction. There is probably more tolerance for murder than for betraying the trust of the faction.

When we are told that our mission is to work as groups to find proof that some faction leaders are somehow being compensated to betray the trust of their people, we know that if this is true, it is a secret they are willing to kill to hide.

The tip we receive is reportedly from a top-ranking official in Divinus. The official remains anonymous, but the document sent to the newsroom reportedly bears the official seal of their faction.

After the instructions are given, the news director wishes us luck. Without prompting, each group huddles under its respective letter to hatch a plan.

"There's no time to waste," says James.

"But where do we even begin?" asks Titan.

"Where else?" James replies, pulling his laptop out of his bag. We all follow suit, pulling out our own laptops.

James shares a digital document with us. "Let's make a list of anyone who could possibly be involved with a scheme like this—their titles, contact information, and close connections."

Then he shares another document with the group. "In this document, everyone needs to list any of their contacts within Divinus. Then, Ray, I want you to cross-reference these lists with any social network you can think of. See if these contact lists are in any way connected."

I start to feel useless. I want to take charge and prove myself, but I'm still in shock at how sharply the stakes of this test have risen. I feel terrified—not so much about the test, but about feeling unprepared.

Soon, names begin to populate the first list: Michelle Robinson, 35, former Divinus faction leader, forced to resign by the current leader after he accused her of having an affair with her secretary. Nathan Widum, the Divinus policy secretary, reportedly bitter toward the current leader, Joshua Welsh, for divorcing his sister and remarrying another woman—making his sister "unfit" to marry anyone else in the faction. Jaleesa Brown, the secretary who mysteriously weathered the scandal with Robinson and even seemed to receive a promotion after Welsh gave a speech on "forgiveness and the Christian way." David Uberman, the Divinus financial minister, who insists his massive fortune—complete with a luxury home and several high-end vehicles—is a reflection of God's favor. "Favor isn't fair," he often tells those who ask, while adding that they should try praying more and being more grateful for what God has given them. The list goes on.

"Okay," says Ray, "I have the cross-referenced list and some people who might be able to connect us to folks who can confirm this tip. I guess we can divide the names up and start meeting with them."

"If, in the course of investigating, we see one another on the outside, we shouldn't tip people off to the fact that we know each other," says James. "As soon as we leave these walls, we are strangers. Gather as many facts as possible before regrouping and taking on the head honchos. We're looking for a leaker—someone more loyal to the faction than its leaders. This is tricky in Divinus, since many leaders convince members that God has chosen them."

I close my eyes and let out a deep sigh, taking in the mission lying ahead of me.

"Are we boring you?" James snaps at me.

"N-no," I stammer, immediately regretting how unsure I sound.

"Good," James replies, his eyes slightly narrowed. "We only have three days—probably less, because we need to stay ahead of the other groups, not behind. As more of us move in, Divinus members will grow more suspicious. Which means the likelihood of one of us getting jailed or killed also increases."

"So let's get this show on the road," says Titan, breaking the tension between James and me.

I grab my pack and list and head out of the building.

It's snowing. It has been snowing for over six months now. People grow more anxious each year as winters stretch longer and longer. Every year, the city seems to be setting new records for winter weather.

All around the city, there are reminders of the crash. Abandoned cars with smashed windshields and missing radios line the streets. Stray cats and dogs roam in search of food. Looking up, I see broken windows and rusted fire escapes on apartment buildings.

Then there's the homeless—hundreds of people living in tent communities with fires burning around the city. Every small enclave where parks used to be has turned into a tent city. Fountains tourists once admired have become bathrooms for many of the homeless. As I walk into the night, I can feel eyes on me. I pull my hood over my head to appear more intimidating.

"Look like the kind of person who makes others cross the street when they see you," my uncle once told me.

This is nothing new to me. I have walked these streets many times before, picking up trash so my uncle and I could have something to sell. But the separation from this reality—living and working in the newsroom—has been jarring. It suddenly hits me how desperate I am to pass this test.

After some internal deliberation, I change the plan. There's no time to gather information. I need to find Michelle Robinson, the former Divinus faction leader. She seems like my best bet to learn more about what's really going on in the faction. They betrayed and rejected her—maybe she'll do the same to them. And if the rumors about her vices are true, she clearly doesn't mesh well with Divinus anyway.

Like many in Divinus, Robinson's personal life is a mystery. But in some of the public interviews she's given, it came out that she's a fan of high-end luxury massage parlors. Most people from Divinus hang out in Ward 4, so I figure I should try to find a luxury spa there.

First, I need a place to sit down, surf the internet, and make some calls. Across the street, I see a coffee shop with one guard holding an AK-47 in front. This is how many businesses stay in service—keeping the unwanted poor and homeless out. I show the guard my Station 7 ID, and he gestures for me to enter.

I open my laptop and start searching for luxury massage parlors in Ward 4.

"Hey, I know you," a teenage girl with dark skin and curly hair nudges me.

"I—I'm sorry," I reply, confused. I'm certain I've never seen her before.

"I follow you online. You work at Station 7, right?" she says.

I'm stunned—slightly afraid, but also flattered. It's a strange experience being recognized after spending most of my life alone and almost invisible.

"Uh, yes, I do," I reply.

"Good luck! You're my favorite! I hope you take over the station," she says with a full smile and a look of excitement.

"T-Thanks," I stammer.

Before I can object, she takes my picture with her phone and walks away. I stare after her for a second, then decide I don't have time to waste.

There's only one luxury spa in Ward 4. I should have known. After the crash, not many people have funds for high-end anything. I write down the address, put on my coat, and head toward the nearest bus stop.

But as soon as I step outside, I see two men in my peripheral vision walking toward me. My heart starts to race, and I immediately pick up the pace.

"*Stupid*," I think to myself. I left that fancy coffee shop and should have hopped directly into a cab. I frantically feel for my pocket knife and pepper spray. The footsteps behind me quicken.

I know I can't outrun them, so I turn around, pull out a knife, and lock eyes with them. That stops them in their tracks. Maybe they were hoping to surprise me.

One of the men immediately takes an attack stance. The other smiles and raises his hand, like he's about to crack a joke. But then I start yelling and charging toward them. I stab the smiling man twice in the leg. Then I swiftly turn around and use my other hand to pepper spray the second guy, who seems unsure whether to attack me or help his friend.

I don't stay to see what happens next. I just run—leaving them in their shock. I sprint several blocks and turn a corner until they're out of sight and I can no longer hear their screams.

Voluntary or not, I'm annoyed that I already seem to be drawing so much attention to myself. I need to get this mission done and get out quickly. After two unsuccessful attempts, I finally hail a cab.

"Take me to First Temple Church in Ward 4," I tell the driver. I decide it's best not to head directly to the spa. One, because I don't want the driver to think I have a lot of money. Two, because I don't think I can afford to stay at such a place for more than an hour.

I glance at my reflection in the cab's rearview mirror. I look terrible. If I want to get into a place like that, I need to look the part. I brush my hair, use a cloth to wipe the sweat off my face, and put on some lipstick.

"Going somewhere special?" the cab driver grins at me through the rearview mirror.

"No," I reply, trying to discourage small talk. I suddenly notice his radio is tuned to Station 7.

"Can you turn that up?" I ask, softening my tone.

"Oh, yeah," the driver responds. "It's the only news I trust."

"Did you hear? Earlier they were reporting that Nathan Widum, the Divinus policy secretary, is considering resigning. Those motherfuckers are all crooks if you ask me. Oh, sorry—those are your people, right?"

"Those aren't... my people," I reply.

"Then why are you going to First Temple?" He looks confused.

I want to end the conversation, but then it suddenly hits me—the news about Nathan Widum may have come from one of the other groups in the field seeking this story.

"Did the report say how they knew he was considering resigning?" I ask, dodging his question.

"I don't really remember," the driver says, shaking his head. "I think it was an anonymous source or something like that. But I believe them. Station 7 is the only true thing in this world full of phonies."

My phone buzzes. I have several messages from James.

"Is this your low profile?!?!?!?!?" reads the message, followed by an image of me in the coffee shop on social media.

"*Shit*," I think to myself.

"**They can trace you and all of us good enough without the social posts**," reads another message. "**They know you're out and about now. You better watch your back.**"

I decide not to reply.

Suddenly, the car slows down and stops in front of a beige building. It's larger than most of the surrounding homes, clearly designed to stand out from the old but well-maintained neighborhood buildings.

"We're here," the driver says, snapping me out of my thoughts.

"Don't worry," he adds as I start to open the door. "I don't judge people for their work at Heavenly Masseuse. It's hard to make a dollar these days," he says with a wink.

"I don't know what you're talking about," I reply, stepping out of the cab. I pay the fee and walk in the direction of the church until he drives away. Then I promptly turn and head toward the massage parlor, Heavenly Masseuse.

The interior of the building is newer and more lavish than the outside suggests. The furniture has vintage designs, though it's all new, with velvet seats. Pink floral wallpaper covers the walls. A podium stands at the front entrance.

"Can I help you?" asks the woman behind the podium.

I haven't thought much about my plan beyond getting here, but the taxi driver gave me an idea.

"Uh, yes," I reply. "I'd like to get a job application."

"I'm sorry, we're not hiring at the moment," she replies with a slight smile, looking completely unapologetic.

"Don't be silly, Savannah," says another woman, walking up behind her and pulling out a paper from behind the podium. "She came all the way here from... where, dear? Where have you come from?"

"Ward 1," I reply, taking the paper and pen she hands me.

"All the way from Ward 1—she can at least fill out an application," the woman says, giving Savannah a coy look. Then she walks away.

Just as I begin filling out the papers, unsure of what my next move will be, the door opens.

"Lady Robinson, you're early!" Savannah says, startled.

My heart thumps in my chest as adrenaline rushes through my veins. I slowly tilt my head up, and there she is.

"I've told you this before, Savannah—call me Michelle," says Robinson.

I've found her. I can hardly contain my excitement. I don't think I've ever been so happy to be in the presence of a possible faction traitor. I go back to filling out the application, this time more slowly and meticulously, to avoid drawing attention to myself.

"I didn't realize I was early," says Robinson, turning to a young woman who enters with her, carrying several bags. "Renee, what time is my next appointment? And why are we early?"

The young woman opens her mouth to offer an explanation.

"Never mind. I don't want to hear your excuses. Savannah, is there no one available who can do this massage? I have an important meeting after this and must be on my way."

Savannah fumbles through the papers on her desk.

"I'm available," I say, trying to sound confident.

Savannah's eyes widen in panic, then she quickly regains her composure.

"Yes...," she pauses, clearly struggling to remember my name.

"Feonix," I pipe up.

"Yes, Feonix is available. But she's new. Is that all right?" asks Savannah, forcing a smile.

"Whatever. Let's get this show on the road," says Robinson, tossing her coat onto her assistant, Renee.

Savannah leads us to a back room, giving me a look that says, *You better not fuck this up.*

"Here you are," she says, opening a door and gesturing for us to enter.

As soon as Savannah leaves, my heart races. It's just Michelle and me in a private room. I can ask her anything. I decide to ease into it.

"I'll give you a moment to change into this robe," I say, stepping out of the room. Three minutes later, I return.

Michelle is under the sheets. The room is warm, almost like a sauna. Soft music plays in the background. Candles flicker on every surface. It's not exactly the scene for an interrogation, but maybe that's for the best.

I pull the sheets away from her back and pour warm oil onto her skin—clearly too much, but only I can tell. Her eyes are closed, and her breathing is heavy.

I remember my dad giving my mom massages when she was pregnant with my little sister. He mostly pressed down on her lower back, center back, and shoulders—places she said she felt pain. I try to imitate his moves on Robinson's back, but it must be clear to her that I'm a novice.

"Can you add more pressure?" she asks after a few minutes.

I try again, and it must be better because her muscles finally start to relax. My mind races. I need a smooth way to ease into this conversation, but nothing comes to me.

"I have lots of tension in my thighs," she says after about 15 minutes.

"Oh, okay," I stammer. I cover her back with the sheets and notice oil spots bleeding through the fabric. Then I pull the sheet off her legs and pour more warm oil. As I rub her thighs, she shifts and moans slightly, widening the space between her legs.

"A little higher," she says, spreading her legs further apart.

My heart races faster as I remember what the cab driver said about Heavenly Masseuse. Did everyone know something about this place that I didn't?

"You can use your fingers or something else if you have it," she says.

That's when I notice she isn't wearing underwear. I freeze. I don't have any more time to waste. Ideas of what to ask her race through my mind until I finally blurt everything out at once like word vomit.

"Is Nicholas resigning because he knows who is taking money from the Saudis? Did he refuse to be involved? Why is he leaving?" I ask, my face stern and serious.

Michelle's body tenses all over. Her eyes widen with fear as she slowly turns her head to look at me. She pushes my hands away from her thighs, pulls the sheets over her body, and stares at me speechless.

"Wh-who are you?" she stammers.

"Look, my story has nothing to do with you—a married faction leader attending massage parlors that double as brothels—yet," I say, pulling a pen, recorder, and notepad from my bag while keeping my eyes on her. "I want to know what's going on with the Saudis. Who are they paying? How are they paying them? When did this start?"

"You work for Station 7," she says, looking at my face for confirmation. "These questions could get us both killed."

"I already asked. Now it's time to talk," I say, hitting record on my device.

"I don't know anything about this," she says, trembling.

"You're lying. Tell me what I need to know, and you'll never see me again. No one has to know we spoke. You simply came here to get your... massage, like you always do."

"Nicholas would never betray the faction. But maybe he knows too much now. You can't cite me as a source!" she blurts out.

"Keep your voice down," I whisper forcefully. "I don't need to cite you if you can lead me to someone who can be cited."

She trembles beneath the sheets, looking at me like I'm her worst nightmare come to life.

"You can't make it in Divinus faction leadership unless you embrace some corruption. But the deal with the Saudis clearly took things too far," she says, looking down at her hands.

"I think Welsh is a plant from another faction. I had my fair share of vices, but I never betrayed the faction like he and David—and maybe now Jaleesa—have," she whispers, her voice pained at the mention of Jaleesa.

"David Uberman, the financial minister, and Jaleesa Brown, the secretary," I confirm, writing their names down.

"Yes," says Robinson.

"How does the money come in?" I ask.

Michelle explains that there is a nonprofit real estate developer specializing in education facilities. The developer takes in donations from around the world, including large sums from the Saudis, to build new schools.

In the city, tax funds normally go toward building and maintaining educational facilities, but tax collection slowed significantly during the crash. In its place, nonprofits and philanthropies—often run by billionaires—took over the role of providing public services.

Since much of the money for public services comes from private entities, the government raised the ceiling for public-private contract disclosures to $500,000 five years ago. It's an absurdly large amount, but with a shattered economic system, people clung to anything that offered stability. Many were so disillusioned they barely noticed that the high ceiling created the perfect environment for corruption.

Michelle continues, explaining that the education developer exploits those loopholes to contract with private companies run by friends and relatives of Divinus leadership. The contracts cover construction, school supplies, custodial services, lunches, and more—all at astronomical prices.

"So, money from the Saudis goes to the schools. The schools contract with ridiculously expensive vendors, who are often related in some way to Divinus leadership. Then, when the vendors are paid, they funnel the money back to Divinus leadership?" I ask, confirming what I heard.

"Exactly," Robinson replies. "Check the campaign finance reports. Anyone receiving support or donations from vendors that could also service a school is probably getting Saudi money under the table, too."

"Look, as far as anyone knows, you got your... massage and said nothing about this. As long as you keep it that way, I will, too. Who can I talk to? Who will go on record?"

"Maybe the school principal at Riverside Academy," Robinson says, pulling the sheet tighter around herself. "He's been uncomfortable with the whole operation, and they're actively trying to replace him—if you know what I mean. To my knowledge, he should be there today."

At that, I gather my things and leave the room. Savannah looks puzzled as I head toward the exit without so much as a glance in her direction.

"Feonix, come back," she calls after me.

I don't stop or turn around. I hail a taxi and get in.

"Take me to Riverside Academy," I tell the driver, relieved that this one isn't as chatty as the last.

I check my phone: seven missed calls from Ray. Through an encrypted app, I send a message to the group.

"Headed to Riverside Academy. I think I have the lead I need to tell this story," I type and hit send.

"WHERE HAVE YOU BEEN?!?"

"We've been trying to reach you!"

"The school???" James messages in rapid succession.

"That's funny," Titan texts. **"I got a bunch of contracts between that school and a custodial company from a source. They're making millions."**

My heart races with a mix of anxiety and excitement. I'm on the right path. The earlier messages disappear automatically. I upload my recording of the conversation with Michelle to my drive.

"You all won't believe what I got Michelle Robinson to say on tape. I'll tell you when we meet tonight," I text.

"In the meantime, Titan and Ray, can you find out who owns the custodial company? See if they have any ties to Divinus

leadership. James, can you check the tax forms from the school and see who its donors are?"

"**Ok**," they all respond.

For a second, my heart swells. I've taken a chance and almost have everything I need for the story—two days ahead of the deadline.

"*As soon as I speak to this principal,*" I think, "*I'm heading back to the newsroom to write one of the most thrilling investigative pieces I've ever written.*"

Ten minutes later, I don't see the window shatter, but I hear it. I hardly notice the driver's blood and brains spray onto my body like a sprinkler system. I just remember screaming as every muscle in my body tenses. I stretch out my arms, gripping anything that can orient me as the taxi spins out of control.

It feels like the world is moving in slow motion. I know the only way the vehicle will stop is if it collides with something.

Then everything goes dark.

4

Behind Faction Walls

I had a flashback to the moment when I woke up in a hospital bed after my family was burned alive. But this time, I know I'm not in a hospital bed.

"We need to get to a hospital," says the male voice holding up my body.

Pain throbs through my body as if someone took a hammer and smashed my muscles. Half of my body is held up by the stranger, while my legs still feel the cold ground beneath them.

I try to speak, but all I can let out is a groan.

"Relax." I realize the voice is familiar, but I can't lift my head to see who it is. "I am going to get you out of here."

Then everything goes black again.

***

The next time I wake up, I'm in a bed, but it isn't a hospital.

I look at my hands—no more blood. I'm wearing a shirt I don't recognize. Footsteps approach, and my heart races, fearful of who's coming.

"I'm glad you're awake," says Emre. I look up to see him speaking to me. "We don't have much time. A day has already gone by. How are you feeling?"

"Where am I?" I ask, feeling a bit disoriented by his familiar face.

"This is my apartment. I brought you back here after finding your body on the ground outside of Riverside Academy. The cab driver..." He pauses. "He didn't make it."

"How did you know I was at the school?" I ask.

"I didn't. I guess we must have been chasing the same tip," he replies.

Then I remember Michelle Robinson at the massage parlor and the principal I was supposed to meet. I need to get back to the station to show my team what I have.

"Where is my bag? I need to get going." It takes all my strength to raise my body and turn my head to look around the room.

"I didn't see a bag," Emre replies. "Actually, I was going to take you to the hospital when I realized that what may have happened was no accident."

My body shudders as I remember the sound of multiple gunshots, the wet sprinkle of blood and brains all over me, and the crash. But I have no idea who tried to kill me. Did Michelle call someone to tell them to kill me? Did they trace me through the photo online? Who took my things? Did I fall into a trap?

"No, it was no accident," I say softly.

"Look." Emre sits on the edge of the bed and gently raises my head so our eyes are interlocked. His hazel eyes seem to pierce through mine. "I've been watching you, and it's no secret that you're smart. I can help you, but you have to help me too. I think if we put what we have together, we can create a story for the station."

"And I can help you through the next two parts of this exam," he continues. "I've taken this test twice before, and I know what it takes to get through it."

"Why should I trust you?" I narrow my eyes at him and move his hand away from my face. "You're not on my team, and in the end, only one of us will be chosen."

"So why not make it one of us? I saved your life, didn't I?" Emre replies, shifting to the rickety chair beside the bed. "Plus, I can tell you from experience that it's almost impossible to get through this on your own. And I don't want to point out the obvious, but right now you need me more than I need you."

"If I'm so useless, then why do you need me? Why trust me?" I snap back.

"'Need' is the wrong word," Emre replies calmly. "I don't need you. But I do trust you. I've

62

been watching you for a while, and you're different from the other... drones at the station."

"Drones?" I repeat quizzically.

"Yes, drones. Those who move, breathe, and live for Station 7," Emre's tone turns dark. "It may not be official, but Station 7 is the largest, most powerful faction there is. They make or break faction leaders, can drive the public to revolt, and do a bunch of other crazy shit."

"You're talking crazy." I shake my head at him.

"And most people working in Station 7 worship it, assuming they're doing God's work or something," he continues.

"And you don't?" I interrupt. "Think you're doing good work, I mean?"

"We live in a time where 'good' is arbitrary," Emre replies. "If 'good' means helping one of the most powerful entities in the city consolidate power and influence over the people, then sure. We're doing good work."

"What do you mean?" I reply. He really sounds crazy to me.

"Look, I enjoy the work Station 7 does just as much as the next guy. If there are faction leaders taking money from foreign governments to deceive the public, then we should expose those fuckers," he says. "But you need to pay attention to the patterns. I guess it would be hard for someone who's only a contractor to see..."

"Excuse me?" I give him a sharp look. "I'm here, aren't I?"

"You're right. I'm sorry," he says.

Emre explains that Station 7 has friends and enemies. The stories station leadership chooses to pursue—and the ones they don't—are not by accident. By breaking up faith in faction leaders, the station builds faith in itself. If we check the history, many of the big investigative stories we produced on leadership were about people who lobbied against the station or ideas the station leadership opposed.

He believes that though many of the station leaders began as journalists with strictly editorial missions, that changed some time ago. Now, many of them take on the role of reformers. They're no longer satisfied with just telling what is; they want to shape what could be.

"You know why I want to be the news director?" Emre's eyes lock onto mine intensely. A smile—or a smirk—creeps onto his face. His broad shoulders hunch over me in the bed. "Because that's the only way I can make this story public. It's time someone checked the largest power in the country."

My mind races. I'm scared and want to shrink. For years, I've worked with an idea of what I thought was the truth. It centered me. It gave me purpose. I don't want to throw a monkey wrench into that vision.

"Y-you're a liar," I yell, hating that my voice stammers. "How do you think you know all this?"

Emre gets up and pulls a projector and a laptop out of the closet. He connects both devices with a black cord and plugs in the projector. The computer's interface becomes visible against the white wall, shown through the light emanating from the projector.

"I've been following this for almost two years now," he says. "Remember Brian Reynolds?"

Emre pulls up his picture on the screen.

"The former Opes faction policy advisor?" I ask.

"Yes," Emre replies. "As you know, Opes believes in trying to achieve pure capitalism—almost anarchy of sorts. So when Station 7 reported that Reynolds was giving contracts to family members, he was forced to resign. Great story, right?"

"Respectable," I reply.

"Well, what people didn't know was that Station 7 employees—those going through tests like us—found several members of Opes leadership doing the same thing Reynolds did. Fortunately for them, they voted in favor of legislation to increase the information war budget," he continues.

Emre scrolls through documents on the screen like he's giving a million-dollar presentation at a company meeting. Each document tracks how different leaders who favored changes like increases to the information war budget, food and resource supply pipelines that included the station, and maintaining media and internet connections that didn't censor the station received favorable coverage. Meanwhile, others were brought down by one scandal or another.

Additionally, he shows documents proving that many who weren't brought down by scandals engaged in similar or worse crimes that were never revealed.

"I tracked this most closely during the last test I took," Emre says, pulling up another document onto the screen. "One of our teammates found multiple faction leaders in the Patriots plotting to attack Latus, the liberals, for their goods like they did nine years ago. Latus isn't as strong as it was before, but they've been trying to rebuild their faction."

When Emre says this, I feel my heart stop. I don't want him to continue.

"But this time, the Patriots want to wipe Latus out," he says, his eyes blazing with an intensity I've never seen before. "A girl named Lynn got hold of the plans and shared them with me before she turned them in for a story. Only the money laundering portion of the documents was published, taking down two faction leaders. There were at least ten involved! The story was much larger, and they knew it! Lynn never got the other parts of the Aptitude test, and later, she disappeared!"

Eight other Patriot leaders planned to attack my old faction again—and they got away with it? They never found the girl? My mind races.

"What do you mean she disappeared?" I ask, desperate for an answer.

"Exactly that," Emre says, his eyes dropping to the floor. "I hadn't seen or heard from her since the test. It's impossible to understand how someone could just disappear like that. Maybe she left for her own good, or maybe something worse happened. The truth is, I don't know."

"What do you get from exposing all of this?" I ask. "You could be the next one to disappear—or me! No one cares about two people disappearing in a world like this! Why are you doing all of this?"

Emre is silent for a moment. I can almost feel the tension in the air between us.

"Right now, you're freaked out because you're beginning to realize you've been living a lie," he says. "I've known that feeling for four years now. Two years ago, I decided I couldn't live like that anymore. Ignorance is fucking bliss, but I don't have that luxury anymore. The truth taunts me to do the right thing, Feonix."

"That's all fine and noble until you're dead," I reply with a sneer.

"But Feonix, what exactly are you living for anyway?" he asks, looking straight at me.

There's silence, as if I could answer such a question. I think of my family, my promise to my uncle, and my need to learn if there was anything else behind my family's murder. I'm fulfilling promises. But do I even know what I'm getting myself into? I have no one. A sick feeling creeps up inside me. The mystery—what was my dad working on? What did he know? Was he one of the leaders seeking to stand up to the station? Could the station somehow be connected to my family's death?

Without faith in Station 7's work, I feel like I have no purpose. I want tears to come to my eyes, but the emptiness I feel in this moment is a pain I know tears won't relieve. My mind teeters on the edge of consciousness, where some people choose death, and others choose madness. Right now, I don't know how those who reach that edge bring themselves back to stability again.

"Emre, I cannot do this," I say, dropping my head into my hands in shame. "This mission seems like something worth pursuing, but I'm not the right person for it."

"Look, I know it's a lot to take in right now, but I want you to think about it," he says, brushing my hair out of my eyes. "When I look into your eyes, I see a determination I don't see in others. I don't know what drives you, but you operate with direction and purpose. You move like something greater than just the station's goals drives you."

"And here I was thinking your looks meant something totally different," I say, smirking up at him, trying to pull myself out of the hole I've sunken into.

"Trust me, this wasn't exactly the first scenario I imagined us in—with you in my bed, I mean," he says, smiling back at me and starting to gather his things.

I narrow my eyes at him and lose the smirk.

"Hey, it's not my fault that the perfect person for this mission also happens to be the most beautiful," he says, not looking at me as he puts the projector back into the closet.

I don't know how to respond. How did we go from talking about a mission that could kill us both to flirting like this?

Then he starts toward the door.

"Emre, where are you going?" I yell after him.

"To sleep. We have to get back to the station first thing in the morning if either of us wants a chance at winning," he replies from the hallway.

"You don't have to do that," I yell back.

"Don't have to do what?" he replies.

"Sleep," I say hesitantly, "on the couch."

What am I doing? I think. I can't believe I just invited him to share a bed with me. But the memory of my family's loss, and maybe my purpose, leaves me feeling so empty and alone. I'm not sure I believe or even care about Emre's mission, but I don't want to be alone at this moment. And I know he doesn't either.

"There's only one bed," he says, poking his head through the doorway, confirming he understands what I'm suggesting.

"I know," I offer him a weak smile and attempt to make space for him beside me.

I can see him studying me.

"Look, I'm not suggesting..." I pause. "I'm not suggesting anything will happen. Just, I don't want to be alone."

My own admission of vulnerability surprises me. But it's true. I've spent so much of my life alone. I miss trusting people. I miss hugs.

He steps into the room with a smirk on his face. I smile back. He dives into the sheets next to me and starts laughing.

"Hey!" I yell. "Don't break the bed! This is the only one you have!"

I hit him with a pillow and chuckle. It almost doesn't sound like me. I haven't laughed in so long. He turns around and leans over me in the bed.

"Maybe I was wrong about one thing, Feonix," he says, scanning my eyes. His face is so close to mine, I can feel the warmth of his breath on my lips. I see my chest moving up and down as the intensity of our breathing increases.

"I'm scared," he continues. "Because I don't think I can do this mission on my own. I said I didn't need you, that 'need' was the wrong word, but I was wrong. I do need you."

My body shudders at the thought of the mission again. Somehow, in the course of this day, I've gone from needing no one—living independently for years—to needing him too. And with my motivation for living mostly destroyed in a matter of hours, I know I need him and this mission to pull myself away from the edge of insanity. But I still can't bring myself to say it.

I look back into his eyes towering over mine.

At that, Emre leans in, and I kiss his lips. He kisses me back. Then I pull myself out from under him. Emre hesitates, not sure what to do at that moment.

"Good night, Emre," I say, turning away from him.

"Uhhh... good night," he replies, slowly turning the other way.

I can still feel the warmth of his back against mine. That's what I need. I listen carefully as the pace of our breathing slows down.

I'm sure I wouldn't have been the first Station 7 worker he's slept with if I had gone through with it, just like he wouldn't have been my first. Something about station workers living and working side by side every day seems to breed an environment where casual intercourse is normal. But being with Emre feels different. There's nothing casual about how desperate we both feel at this moment, and I pray I've made the right decision.

5

Secrets in the Snow

It couldn't have been more than four hours into the night when I hear something jingling at the doorstep. Someone is trying to get inside the apartment. My heart races.

I shake Emre awake and press my finger to his lips, signaling for him to be silent. He must see the terror in my eyes because his sleepy disposition quickly changes to someone who is up and alert.

He gets up and frantically puts on his winter clothes while I scramble for my own. While he's getting dressed, I notice several unusual tattoos on his inner left thigh, but there's no time to think about it. We hear the door creak open along with some whispering. Emre throws a jacket over me and points to the window. I quickly zip up the jacket and open the window.

The cold winter air prickles my face as I climb out onto the rusty fire escape. Emre hands me his keys and goes back inside.

"Where are you going?" I whisper, frantic and panicked.

"My bag, my laptop," he whispers back.

"There!" a man yells and starts running in our direction.

I look up to see Emre's bag flying out the window. Then I hear what sounds like a punch and a door slamming.

"Go!" Emre yells, climbing out the window after me. "The blue car in the corner—start it!"

I jump off the ladder and run toward the car. My legs throb with pain. The keys fumble in my hands as I try to find the right one. My heartbeat races, and my legs ache from the leap. After what seems like an eternity, I manage to get inside the car and start it.

I haven't driven a stick shift in a long time and am not sure I still know how. I place my hand on what I remember to be the gear and move the stick to reverse. The vehicle jerks backward, hitting the car behind it. I wince, hoping there isn't too much damage.

I see someone running toward me in the alley. As we make eye contact, the person pauses and begins to pull what appears to be a weapon from their pocket. I glance up at my rearview mirror and see Emre slowing the pace of his run, his eyes locked on the guy in front of me. Above him, another man climbs down the fire escape to catch up with us.

With shaky hands, I move the car gears from reverse to drive and press my foot down on the accelerator, steering directly into the body of the man in front of me. I think I hear a crack as the car makes contact with his body. Quickly, I shift gears into reverse, sending his body sliding off the car. I stop the car next to Emre, and he jumps into the passenger seat.

"Go!" he yells.

I shift gears back into drive and press my foot down on the gas, sending the car skidding on ice for about four seconds until I regain control and speed away. I can see the figure of a man in the rearview mirror drop a gun he was aiming at our car as we disappear into the night.

"Where should we go?" I ask, my voice shaking.

"Let's get to the station. We've wasted too much time," Emre replies, letting out a heavy sigh. "Who do you think is after you?"

"I'm not sure, but only Michelle Robinson knew where I was headed when you found me after the crash," I reply.

"Do you think there's a reason for her to try to kill you?" he asks.

"Apart from the fact that I cornered her into divulging Divinus' biggest secrets? I don't know. Why were you at the school?" I ask, trying to flip the questioning. I'm still not sure I can fully trust him—or anyone else at this point.

"I met with the principal of that school a few hours earlier at another location in the city. He gave me some pretty valuable information about the foreign money coming in," he replies.

"I was supposed to meet him at the school to pick up some supposedly damning contracts, but when I got there, he was gone, you were on the ground, and I figured something was wrong."

"Did you record the first interview with the principal?" I ask.

"Yes," he replies with a smile. "But I'm worried that our interview might have gotten him killed." His smile falls.

"People start to mark Station 7 employees once they learn who you are. They like to know who's talking to them, what their habits are—especially people with something to hide. After my last test, I had people going through my trash to find more information or dirt on me."

"Are you serious?" I ask, shocked.

"I couldn't believe it," he says, pausing to gaze out the window. "But I guess it makes sense. If they can't find something wrong with your story, it's time to go after your character."

We pull up to the gate surrounding Station 7 around 3:30 a.m. A machine scans my eyes, and the gate opens for us to drive in.

I wonder how I'm going to explain my absence to my team when they wake up in the morning or how I'll convince them to work together with Group A to get the story done. But at that moment, I'm more tired than anything.

Both Emre and I crash as soon as our heads hit the pillows in my tiny space.

6

Against the Clock

It seems as though the instant we fall asleep, it's time to wake up.

"For now, I guess it's best we don't act like we know each other," says Emre.

I nod in agreement. He leaves the room first. I change into another t-shirt and jeans, then go to meet my team.

"Oh shit, Feonix, you're alive," exclaims Ray. "I guess you'll have a good explanation for this because James is pissed."

"I don't have to answer to anyone," I snap back at Ray. "I'm here now."

"No, I think you owe us an explanation," says James. "We're at the deadline, and I feel like we have enough to do this story without you."

"It's true," echoes Titan. "We have contracts. We have interviews. We know who owns the limited liability corporations behind the contracts."

"I was almost killed for that information. You'd have never found that out without me," I say, unwilling to give in or appear weak.

"Almost killed?" asks Ray. "After two days, you could at least tell us what happened. Where were you?"

"I can't believe this is what you want to waste our limited time going over. They fucking tried to kill me, alright? I was on the street! Left for dead," I yell. Hot pangs of anger rise in me. I feel overwhelmed with emotion, and I want to cry, but my pride won't let the tears fall.

I don't know why answering their questions annoys me so much. Something about it seems to diminish my role in getting the story done. I should be leading this group, I think, not James.

James pulls out his laptop.

"Let's move on," he says, studying my disposition. "We have a story to write and not much time to write it. Did you get all the interviews you needed?"

I shake my head.

"I only got Michelle Robinson's interview," I say.

"Shit," James replies, interrupting me. "We went out to see if we could find you or the principal since we got the contracts. Then, while we were searching, Channel 11 reported that the principal was found dead with a gunshot wound, in what police described as an act of suicide."

His words leave me breathless with fear. Channel 11 is a government-run news channel.

"We were," he pauses, "worried we'd see a report about you next."

James' eyes hover over me for a second. I can see that he's angry but also relieved to see me alive. Something about his stare softens my defensive disposition.

"I know someone from Group A who told me they had an interview with the principal," I say. "Maybe they'll work with us to put together the rest of the story?"

"Why would they do that? Why should we do that?" James asks quizzically. "We have most of what we need, right? And you have Robinson's interview, right?"

"But I told her I wouldn't use it," I reply. "It was technically off the record."

"Was that before or after she tried to have you killed?" asks Titan sarcastically.

"We don't know if it was her, and I can't risk putting another source in danger," I reply. "That principal was trying to do the right thing. That's why he died. And—albeit a bit reluctantly—Michelle might have been trying to do the right thing too."

"Back to my question," says James. "Why should the people from Group A work with us?"

"Because maybe they're missing story parts too," I interrupt. "Worst case scenario, they say no, and we're back where we started."

"Worst case scenario, they say no, and we use Michelle's tape," James says, looking at me sternly.

"Agreed," say Titan and Ray in unison.

I turn away from my group, take a deep breath, and walk toward Group A. I see only three people from their team sitting at a table. Each group normally has four people. They're huddled around a circular table with their laptops open in front of them, but none of them are looking at their laptops. They're yelling at each other.

"Can I help you?" snaps a girl with brown hair as I approach their table. I recognize her face. She's the same girl the news director yelled at after she noted that the test could get us killed.

For a second, I don't know where to start. They look heated, including Emre, who meets my gaze for a second before looking away.

"I wanted to propose something," I stammer. "But I guess it's not a good time?"

"If it's about the test, now is as good a time as any," Emre says, trying not to appear too interested.

"What do you want? We don't have time to waste," says the girl. I see the look on her face fade from anger to something that seems like defeat.

"Look," I try to meet each of their eyes and appear confident as I speak. "We've gathered enough evidence for a pretty strong story," I pause.

"But we're missing some important pieces—pieces that could make the story stronger and maybe even winning. At the end of this round, some groups will be knocked out of the running. But I think if we work together, we might have what you need, and you might help us too," I pause again.

"What makes you think we have the pieces your team is missing?" asks a blonde girl sitting next to Emre.

"Look, I'd rather do this negotiation with your whole team. Is someone from your team not here?" I ask.

Emre sighs. "We don't know where he is." He doesn't meet my eyes when he says it, and I can tell he suspects the worst.

"I'm sorry," I say, looking at the other two on the team. "But we don't have much time. Do you all want to try to make the pieces we have work or not?"

"How would this work?" asks the blonde girl, her blue eyes fixed on mine.

"We would all agree to share a byline, then show each other what we have and write, record, and edit a winning story," I reply.

"Do we even know if this is allowed?" asks the girl with brown hair. "We were assigned to separate groups."

"Don't make rules where there aren't any. We weren't expecting a dead group member," Emre snaps back at the brown-haired girl. "There are clearly few rules, if any, in this shit. I'm in. What do we have to lose?"

He looks back and forth at his other team members. The resolve of the other two seems to give in.

"Where are your other group members?" asks the blonde girl, turning to me.

I turn to look in the direction of my group. Ray types while James and Titan huddle around him. I point in their direction.

Emre begins to gather his things. "Come on, guys. Let's see what they have."

The other two begin to gather their things as well. I want to let out a sigh of relief, but I know this isn't the end. My eyes meet Emre's for a second, and he gives me a slight smile before quickly looking away. My mind flashes back to the night before, wrapped in his arms, his mission. Things seem to be moving so fast, and even though I'm the one moving, I'm not sure if I'm fully in control of it all.

James is the first to notice us approaching. His sudden silence must alert Titan and Ray because soon they are looking up, watching us approach.

"James." He sticks out his hand toward Emre, not waiting for me to introduce him.

"Emre." Emre takes his hand and shakes it.

"Gabby," the brown-haired girl says, extending her hand toward James.

"Alex," says the blonde girl with them.

It's at that moment that I realize I only know Emre's name. Though I'm annoyed at James for not waiting for me to introduce everyone, I'm glad I get their names without having to admit that I didn't ask for them.

After the introductions, we dive straight into the work. Our team has a host of documents—company ownership records, tax filings, and more. In addition, we have Michelle's tape, and though we can't use it for the story, it helps everyone understand how those pieces fit together.

The documents trace the ownership of 14 limited liability corporations that six schools contract with to four officials in Divinus leadership. Seven companies belong to Joshua Welsh, the faction leader who took over after Michelle Robinson was forced to resign. Four companies are owned by David Uberman, the financial minister. Two companies are owned by Jaleesa Brown, the secretary. The last company belongs to someone I'm not familiar with—a woman named Paige Watts, who chairs all the leadership seats but maintains a low profile. Her position is an appointed one. Welsh elected her.

Emre's interview with the principal turns out to be as useful as he described. The principal divulged how he found out about the scheme and what leadership forced him to do. According to the tape, he acted in response to a combination of threats to his family and bribes he received. He breaks into sobs periodically during the recording. I shudder at the thought of his death.

Emre also has photocopies of several school contracts given to him by the principal. Many are between $400,000 to $500,000, just below the forced public reporting amount.

Gabby has another interview with someone she describes as a top official in Divinus. This official wants to remain anonymous but allows their quotes to be used in writing only. Gabby refuses to reveal who it is, saying she took an oath not to reveal the person. James seems anxious about this.

"So far, we have one dead person on the record and one anonymous source. I don't know if that's enough for the kind of charges we're about to bring up," James says, appearing nervous for the first time.

There are only three hours left, and everyone seems to grow more anxious.

"All I have are notes," says Gabby. "The person refused to be recorded, saying it could get them killed. Seeing what happened to Emre's source and one of our teammates, I think that's enough to prove their point."

"We can simply write that the source feared for their life," I chime in.

"I think enough people have died for this story. It's not only enough to publish," I pause, remembering the taxi driver whose brains ended up all over my clothes. "We have an obligation to get this out so their deaths weren't in vain."

"Total, these contracts add up to a whopping $19 million and counting," says Alex. She's a data wizard and has written some code that extracts the data from the contracts and adds it to a spreadsheet.

Titan works with Alex to create video and picture graphics that make her data easy to interpret. The graphics trace the money from the Saudi officials and several other sources through the schools, then through the companies, then through friends and relatives of Divinus leadership, and finally to the leaders themselves. It's an elaborate cascade of images and colorful lines flowing between each group.

We decide to have Emre and Gabby work on the audio narration of the story. The narration will run behind a video Titan is supposed to create for the web and television. It will also run on the radio.

Ray types furiously for the digital text version of the article. James and I are assigned to do the editing. I plan to edit Emre, Gabby, and the data team, while James edits Ray. It's an ambitious goal for the short time we have—two and a half hours left—but we have no choice.

My biggest fear is making a stupid mistake in the story that I don't catch. I know if there are any mistakes, Divinus leadership and anyone else implicated by the story will use it to discredit the whole thing. I wish we had more time, but I know it's better to publish the best we can within the time frame than to do nothing at all.

About an hour passes before Emre and Gabby are ready for me to review their script. For audio stories, the standard practice is to edit by listening. As they speak, I frantically mark up the script, moving parts around and crossing out several lines. They spend about 20 minutes reading the story to me. By the end of my markup, I've cut about five minutes of talking—everything else is essential.

Then I highlight all the facts and divide them between Emre and Gabby to double-check. I send the script to Titan so he can begin making some graphics that will be mixed with the audio to create a video.

Everyone is working frantically.

Soon, Emre and Gabby revise the story. I quickly review it while they record, stopping them and adding small tweaks as they speak. Normally, I'd edit the story one more time before they start recording, but with only an hour left, there just isn't enough time.

We finish before James and Ray, with only 20 minutes left.

"Emre, how's it going?" I try to appear composed as I ask him, but at this point, I'm afraid. I don't know how we'll finish in time. I'm also terrified that there are glaring mistakes I missed. He looks into my eyes, and I can tell he sees my panic. Then he pulls me into a corner away from the others.

"It's going to be okay," he says, scanning my eyes. "Look at me." He puts his hands on my cheeks and gently lifts my face. His hazel eyes lock onto mine.

"We're almost done. I'm going to review the audio with Gabby one more time before we help Titan add it to the graphics." He leans in as if to kiss me, but out of the corner of my eye, I see Gabby staring in disbelief.

I pull away from him. He turns to see Gabby's eyes locked on us, and I quickly walk away, avoiding eye contact with her. I hear him let out a curse before walking toward her. There's no time to explain, no time to argue, but I know it doesn't look good.

I pull out my laptop and enter the document that Ray and James are editing. It's already in the content management system, ready to be published.

"I'll go over this until the time is up. One more edit," I yell in their direction.

They both nod, not bothering to look up from their computers. For a second, as I edit, my mind wanders back to Emre and Gabby. I wonder if he tries to explain or if Gabby does the smart thing and lets it go for now. Then I push the thoughts out of my mind and get back to work.

I look up at the clock—two fuckin' minutes.

"We have to publish now!" I yell.

Titan is literally sweating. I read over two more lines—no mistakes. Then I hop out of the document.

"Time's up!" yells a woman on the stage. It's the same woman who first spoke to us.

"Hurry up and gather around," she says, taking the microphone from the stand on the podium. Then she steps around it, directly in front of us as all the groups gather before the stage. She brushes her curly red hair out of her face.

"Right now, our producers are going through whatever you all have submitted," she continues. "In the end, only one team's story will be published. If your story isn't chosen, your team will be eliminated."

"I thought we had two chances out of three tests," someone from Group D yells.

"We decided to move this process along a bit quicker," the woman says nonchalantly.

Someone from another group begins sobbing. James' hands ball into fists at his sides. I can tell he's struggling to hold back his emotions. So are many others in the room. There's a heaviness in the atmosphere that builds from the fear, frustration, and anger several contestants are trying to suppress. I feel the sweat building behind my ears and in my armpits.

For a moment, my mind flashes back to the tents on the streets and the men who tried to rob me. That will be my life every day if I don't make it to the next round. There will be no way to even consider Emre's mission again. I don't even know if we'll see each other again.

Outside these walls, survival comes first. For many people, survival comes before family and definitely before love—or whatever Emre and I have going on. The conditions of the outside society bring out the worst in us, and I know it. I've lived it once before, which is why I'm terrified of going back.

"Until the producers decide, you're all instructed to get lunch and take a break," says the red-haired woman. "Good luck. Lunch will be in the cafeteria in the room to your left. For some of you, it will be your last meal here."

Then she prances off the stage. Something about the way she moves emphasizes that she doesn't give a shit about the contestants—that she doesn't hear or see the tears in multiple eyes.

I decide to try to pull myself together.

"Guys, I suggest we take the break we're offered," I say, turning to the group. "We have a solid story. People died for the story we gave them. If that isn't strong enough, then I still think we should all be proud, knowing we did our best."

"Easy for you to say, lover-girl," Gabby snaps at me in anger. She points her finger between Emre and me. "You two fuck each other, then you both tried to fuck over us too!"

"What is she talking about?" James looks at me.

"Gabby, it's not wha—" I start, but she quickly cuts me off.

"Oh, you guys didn't know either?" Gabby continues, sounding more hysterical now. "Well, it turns out that these two are an item—secretly working together and dealing behind our backs! We probably won't even make it to the next round. Might get eliminated on a technicality after they convinced us all to work together as a giant group and break the rules!"

"Gabby, calm down," I say, stepping toward her. "I understand. I owe you an expla—"

"Get away from me, you bitch!" she screams, and suddenly I feel her fist make contact with my face, sending my gaze to the ground. I look back up to see her charging at me.

She knocks me to the ground, and soon we're rolling and clawing at each other, each of us trying to overtake the other.

At that moment, the calm composure I've struggled to maintain escapes me. I lose it. Everything I've tried to keep down—my fear, my lack of hope, my feeling of betrayal by the station—bubbles up inside me in the form of rage. And before I realize how badly I've beaten Gabby, I hear Emre's voice yelling at me to stop.

Both Emre and Ray try to drag me away from Gabby, while James and Alex work to pick her up off the ground. She's covered in blood and bruises. As I blink and strain my eyes to focus on her bloodied body, a feeling of horror washes over me. I can't believe what I've done. That I lost control like that. I look at my bruised hand, covered with blood—much of it not my own.

I glance around to see the shocked and horrified expressions on the faces of others in the room as they stare at me.

As soon as I stop struggling, Titan and Emre release their grip on me. Without saying a word, I turn and walk briskly out of the room and into the bathroom. Inside, I search for a toilet, close the door behind me, and vomit.

Then the tears come—tears I've held back since my time in Emre's apartment when he told me the truth about what Station 7 had become. The tears quickly turn to sobs, and when I remember my family and why I came to the station in the first place, I can hardly breathe.

I don't know how much time passes before I hear Emre's voice again.

"Feonix," he says softly.

"Leave me alone," I yell back.

"Okay," Emre replies. "But I wanted you to know Gabby's going to be alright. She's in the infirmary, so you don't need to feel too bad."

Somehow, that news does make me feel a little better.

"Also, the results are in," he pauses, and my stomach churns again. "Our teams are going to the next round."

I can hear the slight smile and relief in his tone.

"You better get some rest and clean up because we start the next test tomorrow. I have a few tips I want to go over with you before it begins," he says through the door.

I almost can't believe it.

"*We won*," I think to myself in disbelief.

I look down at my hands, still bloody and bruised. I imagine how unsettling the sight of me—on the floor, hunched over a toilet—would be to some people. I let rage, panic, and fear take over me and completely lost control.

Suddenly, I'm flooded with shame and embarrassment. What kind of leader allows themselves to lose control like that?

I pull myself off the ground, open the door, and walk toward the sink. In the mirror, I see how haggard I look. I can barely stand to look at myself.

"*Pathetic*," I think.

The outlines of dried tears streak my cheeks. Bags have formed around my eyes, making my exhaustion visible, and a scar is starting to form next to my left eye where Gabby punched me.

I turn on the sink and let the water run for a while before I begin washing my face. I gargle some water and spit it out.

I know I need to release all that mental baggage. Maybe it's better that I lost control for a second. But staring into the mirror at that moment, I know one thing for sure—I'll do everything in my power to never let that happen again.

"I can't lead without control," I think, remembering my uncle's lessons.

7

The Anatomy of a Conspiracy

When I walk out of the bathroom, I see the team in a circle, talking with one another. Gabby and Emre are noticeably absent.

"Hey, Feonix!" Titan waves excitedly. "Come celebrate with us. I just got six thousand more followers!"

I notice they have a pitcher of beer, and they are all drinking. I walk toward them.

"Dude, I sure hope the next part of this test doesn't involve any cage fighting because you could probably beat the shit out of all of us," exclaims Ray with a chuckle.

I roll my eyes and shake my head at him. "Ray—"

"Dude, you beat her ass," he continues, punching his fist against his open palm between each word.

"She had it coming," says Alex before taking another swig of beer. "That girl is bat-shit crazy, and she knew we would have never made it to the next round without you."

Titan hands me a beer.

"It's true," Titan echoes. "We wouldn't have made it past the first round without you. So let's all have a round in Feonix's honor."

I'm shocked and relieved to hear the accolades from the team.

"Guys, we all know everyone chipped in to get this done. It was a group effort," I say.

I hadn't noticed the slight smile creeping onto my face. Then a thought crosses my mind—today these people are my comrades, but tomorrow they will be my competition.

"But we have to keep an eye on you," says James, all red-faced. He's clearly reaching his limit on the beers. He leans in next to me in an attempt to whisper, but what he says is audible to everyone at the table.

"Don't think I don't remember what Gabby said about you and Emre," he laughs.

"Fuck you," says Alex. "She can sleep with whoever she wants to if she can fight and win like she's been doing. Don't think we can't list out a few people you've been caught with. Like we got the morality police in here. If I didn't know any better, I'd say someone sounds a little jealous."

James throws his hands in the air as if surrendering to law enforcement.

"Easy, Alex," he replies. "I am actually making some plans tonight, since it may be our last, if you're interested."

I want to correct them, but I don't see the point.

Alex rolls her eyes and takes another swig of beer. This is my first time seeing James so relaxed and childish. I don't really like it. When I look into his eyes, he quickly turns away from me.

"How did folks from other groups respond when they heard we won?" I ask.

"Dude, it was intense," says Ray. "For those who lost, they already had their belongings packed."

"They didn't even let them go back to the room," chimes in Titan.

"The kind of shit that makes you lose faith in this place," says Alex.

"The kind of shit that reminds me I need to go to bed and prepare for tomorrow," says James. "Tomorrow things will be different."

He stands up. "And Alex, I'd be careful about saying too many statements like that. Good luck, everyone."

James glances at me one more time and then walks away.

"Woah, someone should pull the stick out of your friend's ass," says Alex. "Also, he's clearly jealous of Emre. Hell, I can't say I'm not a little jealous myself."

She smirks at me. I feel heat rising in my face. I'm flattered, but definitely not used to all the attention.

"It was amazing seeing you edit," says Ray. "You really are as good as they say."

"They?" I reply, quizzically.

"Geeze, Feonix, you can keep up with the news about everything in the world and not what people say about you?" Titan responds. "We were super excited to see you on our team because you are known for not missing a thing. And man, did you deliver!"

I smile.

"Do we know what happened to the final story?" I ask. "Did it air? Is it online?"

"I didn't watch the whole thing yet, but I saw some of the reaction on social, and it was bonkers," says Titan.

He pulls out his laptop and turns the screen so we can all see. He hits play on a video from a social website. It shows a crowd gathering outside Divinus headquarters earlier in the day. A line of guards forms in front of the building in response to the crowd. As the crowd grows larger, so does their anger and chants. From the video, we see several people holding up phones, ropes, sticks, and even one or two knives. The crowd pushes forward, clearly outnumbering the guards.

Suddenly, all chaos breaks loose. One guard breaks rank and runs while another opens fire on the crowd. We watch in horror as some people fall to the ground dead while the others attack the guards, quickly overwhelming them. Then, as they pour into the building, a helicopter flies toward the compound. It's clear Divinus' leadership intends to escape, but judging from the video, it's too late. The crowd is already on the roof, hurling insults and objects at the helicopter. It cannot land and is forced to turn away.

"Apparently, they later brought out Joshua Welsh and Paige Watts and hung them," says Titan. "Do you all want to see it?"

"No," I interject. "But why only those two?"

"I don't know," Titan replies.

I look at Ray and Alex, who both shrug.

"Can you pull up the story?" I ask.

I sit next to Titan and scan through the text. There are some edits, which is expected. But when I get to the details about the contracts and money found within them, my heart sinks in terror. There are only eight contracts listed—those belonging to Welsh and Watts. All data, documents, and graphics listing the others owned by David Uberman and Jaleesa Brown are removed.

"Why did they do that?" asks Alex, reading over my shoulder.

I can feel a sense of panic creeping up my spine. I remember what Emre told me about the mission and the girl who went missing on his team after her group's story was published. I turn to the others, and I'm sure they can see the panic in my eyes.

"Guys, promise me you won't ask or tell a soul about what you just saw," I say.

"Why? What's going on? What do you know?" Alex asks defensively.

"Look, it's not safe to talk about this here. I have to go." I stand up and start gathering my things. "I think it's best we all get some rest before the morning."

"Dude, are you alright?" Ray reaches out for my shoulder. I grab his hand before he can touch me.

"Ray, please." I look into his eyes. "Trust me on this one."

I start to walk away. I take one more look back at the team of people I've worked with these past few days. They are the closest thing I have to friends or family at the moment. A pang of sadness creeps over me, knowing that the next day they will be my competition. But there is also a burning anger inside me that slowly turns into rage. I know this time I will control it, direct it where it needs to go—at Station 7.

Station leadership is using and essentially killing contestants to meet their agenda. Many contestants are dying, willingly putting themselves in harm's way, thinking they are fighting for freedom of information, accountability, and rebuilding the fourth estate. But it's all lies. Like the government and billionaire-run outlets, Station 7 has an agenda and is wielding information in deceptive ways to push it forward.

I head straight to my room, where I'm sure Emre is waiting for me. On the way, I see a sign that says infirmary with an arrow. I turn to follow it.

The sign directs me through a narrow stairwell underground and up to a thick gray door. The door opens, revealing a large dark room. As I walk in, the lights respond to my motion and turn on. There are rows of people in what look like egg-shaped capsules lining the walls. Each person has a mask with tubes covering their nose and mouth. The masks appear to help them breathe or maybe keep them asleep.

I want to see Gabby. I don't know why—maybe to make sure she's alright?

In the back of the room, one pod is larger and more elevated than the others. My foolish curiosity draws me nearer, so I walk toward it. When I reach the glass, it becomes clear why the pod is elevated. The news director is inside.

I stare at her, encapsulated in the egg-shaped glass.

So, I think to myself. She really is dying.

For some reason, I think maybe even that fact might be a lie. Maybe the test is something else. Maybe it isn't about finding her replacement at all. But still, something doesn't add up. I always imagined that whoever takes over would spend years in her tutelage before becoming the director. I imagine myself destroying the power to the capsule.

I scan her face. She is thinner than I remember but also strangely familiar. Suddenly, her eyes shoot open. I'm so taken aback that I fall to the ground in fear. I quickly scramble back up and run for the exit, toward the large gray door. Behind me, I hear the sound of her pod opening, but I don't stop to look back.

I faintly hear her yell for me to stop as the door closes behind me. I don't stop. I run until I get to my room. Then I let myself in and slam the door behind me. I drop my hands to my knees to catch my breath.

"Are you alright?" asks Emre, startled.

I slump down to the floor in exhaustion. "I'm not sure." I have to take a breath between each word.

"How could you've possibly had any problems going from the cafeteria to your room?" Emre asks with some sarcasm. "You realize that part of our plan to get the director position requires you to make it to the test."

"Forget it! Let's just focus on the next test," I snap.

"Feonix, out of all the people you will have to fight, I would like to remind you that I am not one of them," says Emre.

"Okay, well, stop the sarcasm," I reply.

"You're right." He reaches out and lifts my head so our eyes meet. "I'm sorry."

"Actually, you were right," I say, turning away from him. "I don't know if I fully believed you when we first spoke, but I saw the final story."

"Wait, what? How?" Emre asks, his face filled with horror.

I explain how we were watching videos on Titan's computer, how we noticed only two people were hung, and all the changes we saw in the story.

Emre looked nauseated.

"I just hope they don't go around talking about what they saw," says Emre.

"I warned them," I reply with a big sigh. "I'm sorry I doubted you."

"No, don't be sorry. I probably would have felt the same way if this was my first time hearing it without direct experience," he says. "Now, let's talk about the next test."

Emre explains that the next test involves a simulation where we will be placed into a virtual world, and only my understanding of truth can help me escape.

"A virtual world?" I respond quizzically.

"Yeah, and somehow the system knows things about you. I think it takes in data from your past—from your behaviors in the station to your online browsing history," he continues. "Any public records that include your name are fodder for the virtual system. To my understanding, it loads terabytes of data on you before you enter."

He says it's paramount that I don't allow old feelings or hidden fears to influence my thoughts. As I listen, I wonder how that's possible with the mountains of fear welling up inside me.

I begin pacing back and forth.

"How am I going to do this with all these thoughts in my head?" I throw up my hands in frustration.

"Don't imagine the truth I have explained; just imagine what they would want you to believe is the truth and follow your instincts that way," Emre explains.

"We really have to get some rest so we're both not delusional tomorrow," he continues. "Come on."

He takes off his shoes and crawls into my twin-sized bed. I pull off my shoes and jeans and crawl into the bed beside him. His body is warm. He turns and wraps his arm over my shoulder so our bodies fit together like two pieces in a game of Tetris. Then he closes his eyes.

"I saw her," I whisper, staring at the white paint chipping in one corner of the ceiling.

"Saw who?" mutters Emre, his eyes still closed.

"Victoria Revel, the director," I reply.

One of Emre's eyes opens, and he looks at me.

"How... where?" he asks in succession.

"The infirmary," I say. "I was looking for Gabby, but then I saw her. She was in one of the healing tubes. She looked really ill."

I turn to look at Emre. He is wide awake and staring at me by this point. The furrow in his brows tells me he is either angry or seriously concerned.

"Does she know you saw her?" he asks.

"I don't know. I don't think so," I reply. "I ran."

"Shit," he mutters under his breath. "They are going to be looking for you tomorrow. If not you, someone who looks like you. Best to change your look a little bit—not too much—and keep a low profile."

"Okay," I say, trying to keep my voice steady.

The thought of Station 7 employees looking for me makes me nervous. I want to sleep, but there are so many thoughts in my head. There's too much I need to make sense of—getting through the next test and the larger mission Emre has now put before me.

After some time, Emre falls asleep. I look at him. It's nice to have a companion, a partner through all this madness. But I can't help wondering if he's more of an asset or a liability.

I pull out my phone and decide to update my followers since that often helps boost support.

We've revealed the truth about Divinus, I start to type. But the statement feels disingenuous, so I delete it.

Onward to Part 2 of the test, I write. Then I hit send.

8

Virtual Reality

I startled awake in Emre's arms. He is shaking me. I don't remember falling asleep.

"We have to get up," he says. "I know it's early, but we need to find you a different look. Not too different, but enough that you can't easily be recognized."

I look in the mirror. My tight curls are held back with a headband, curling together like a small bush at the end.

"I could straighten my hair, but it's going to take some time," I reply.

"Good idea!" Emre says with some excitement. "I can help you!"

"Ugh, I don't know about that," I say, wondering how he would have any idea how to do my hair. Emre's hair is short and straight. "I got this."

"No, you don't understand. I actually learned to do hair to pay for school before," Emre says, giving me a look that tells me he is offended by my doubt.

"My hair is clearly nothing like yours, though," I reply. "I don't think you do hair like mine."

Emre stops gathering his things and looks at me.

"I want you to take a shower, wash your hair, and come out here," he says.

I'm not sure how else to respond, so I just get up and do as he asks. After I wash my hair and take a shower, I sit down in front of him, still in my towel.

Then I am amazed. Emre brushes, combs, blow-dries, and straightens my hair until I almost can't recognize myself. I haven't straightened my hair in years, and even when I did, it was never this nice. I turn my head back and forth so my hair flips from side to side. A big smile creeps over his face.

"I can't believe you did this," I say.

He leans over me and kisses my forehead.

"You look beautiful," he says. "But we need to get ready and get out of here."

This guy is full of surprises. I make a mental note to ask him about his hairstyling abilities another time. We gather our things and head out of my room.

As soon as I step into the hallway, my heart leaps with fear. There are guards all over the place.

"*Emre was right,*" I think. "*He saved me again. They're looking for me!*"

"Relax," Emre whispers. "They're not looking for you. They're looking for the figure the director saw last night."

I think about my new hairstyle and hope it's enough of a change for people not to suspect that I'm the figure. We head toward the room we gathered in before for the tests.

"So, there is something between you two," Alex says, looking between Emre and me as we enter the room together. "What did you do to your hair? Are you both going on dates between the tests or something?"

I decide to ignore her comments. I see Gabby standing with Ray and Titan toward the back of the room. James is in the front with a look of anxiety and seriousness on his face. I can tell he is mentally preparing himself for whatever comes next.

I look around. There are only seven of us left, including me.

"Sorry I'm late," says the exotic-looking woman with tight red curls who first spoke to us as she walks onto the stage. "There was concern that we may have had a security breach. If any of you have information regarding this breach, please let us know. For security reasons, I'll be explaining the directions for this next test."

I can't move. Her words make me freeze, and I don't want to draw any attention to myself. I wonder what will happen if they recognize me. Will I be arrested? Maybe they'll try to understand why I was there. Would they believe me if I told them it's all just an accident? It will surely eliminate me from the test. I can feel my stomach curling inside.

"You all are the lucky few who have made it to the second test," she continues. "This test asks you to find the truth in a world full of lies."

She explains that we will all be placed into a simulation where everything appears real, but only things that are truly real can help us find our way out. The simulation is designed so we can't get out unless we find our way out.

"What do you mean by that?" Ray asks.

"I mean you can't escape the simulation unless you find your way out. You won't be stuck physically, but you might be stuck mentally," she explains. "For some reason—and we haven't quite figured this out yet—because the simulation plays with neurons in your brain, sometimes when we pull people out before they find their own way out, they go mad. It's like they're mentally stuck in the simulation."

"We try to keep people in the simulation as long as possible," she continues. "We've even attached feeding tubes to people so they don't die out here in the real world. But this is why, before you enter the next test, we ask you to sign a waiver stating that after two weeks on the feeding tube, we are allowed to remove it and either let you die naturally or attempt to pull you out of the simulation."

"Da fuck," I hear Titan mumble under his breath.

I glance up at Emre, wondering why he hasn't told me all of this. He doesn't look back at me. A pang of fear and distress creeps through my body, but I know there's nothing left to do but move forward.

We are each handed our waivers—words spelling out exactly what the redhead told us appear on the page. At the bottom, there are two boxes to check. One offers the option of removing the headset with the chance that I might become a crazy person. The second box offers the chance to search for my way out until I die in the physical world.

My hands quiver over the two options. I think about what it would mean to roam the outside world as a mad person—or worse, as a madwoman. I would be homeless, useless, and vulnerable in a destitute world. I could be raped, maybe killed.

"*It is better to die with some dignity,*" I think as I check the box saying I will search until I can't anymore.

At that moment, a resolve rises in me. I know that no matter the stakes in any of these tests, I will face them head-on. Maybe I've known all along that I would never give up. But for me, the stakes definitely change after meeting Emre and learning the truth behind the station. I know that life without passing isn't a life I want to live.

After an assistant gathers our waivers, we are escorted to another room. Inside the small room, there are seven large chairs arranged in an outward-facing circle. The chairs are metal with brown padding on areas where someone's arms, butt, back, head, and legs should rest. Straps hold down a person's arms and legs.

"In the past, some test-takers have hurt themselves as their brains get overstimulated by the simulation," the exotic-looking woman explains.

"You may want to take a restroom break before we get started," she says, gesturing to the corner of the room where there are two bathrooms—one for women and one for men.

We all line up outside the bathrooms. Gabby and Ray go in first.

"What do you guys think?" Alex asks, addressing nobody in particular.

"I think we don't really have a choice," James replies, clearly a little sour about the whole situation.

"Hopefully it's not as bad as it sou—" Emre begins to say.

"We don't all have an alliance," James interrupts, looking back and forth between Emre and me with disgust.

Then I notice the others looking at us with suspicion as well.

"Look," I say, raising my voice. "We all know that there are no alliances when we either pass these tests or die. Emre knows that, and so do I."

I can't look him in the eyes when I say it. I'm afraid that I might have hurt him.

Gabby comes out of the restroom, and I go in. The space is small and dingy. There is one toilet, a sink, and a mirror. It smells as if there's no ventilation system.

I hold my breath, sit on the toilet, and pee. I think about all the people waiting outside.

"*I have to manage my emotions,*" I think to myself. "*It really is too dangerous to get attached to anyone, even Emre.*"

Part of me wants to stay in the bathroom and hide until they come and throw me out. But then the stream of pee turns to a trickle, and I figure it's time to face my next test.

While washing my hands, I catch a glimpse of my reflection in the mirror. My hair is long and flowing, and I remember how Emre woke me up this morning to get it done.

Suddenly, I want to tell him I'm sorry—that I didn't mean what I said while standing in line. I want to tell him I was under pressure and wrong. I want to hug him, kiss him one more time before I die searching for the end of this simulation.

"*But there's no time,*" I think to myself.

I walk out of the bathroom and pick one of the large chairs to sit in. The chairs are so big I have to push my arms down and use my legs to hop off the ground before I'm fully in it. After about 15 more minutes, everyone is seated. Emre sits to my right.

I pick up the headset to my left and hold it in my hands. It reminds me of the clunky virtual reality headsets people used to have before the crash. I glance at Emre. He turns to me as if he feels my gaze.

"It's going to be okay," he mouths.

I nod. There's so much I want to tell him, but I know this isn't the time. Then it occurs to me that the right time may never come. I look back at him. His headset is already on. My heart sinks. I take a deep breath and put on my headset.

As soon as I place the headset on, my entire body stiffens. I feel as if my inner self—maybe it's what I imagine to be my soul—leaves my body and falls through a dark vortex that spans space and time.

When I open my eyes, I'm on the ground in a room I don't recognize. I stand up and dust myself off. The sun is blazing through the windows. I try to get my bearings but still feel confused.

"*Where am I?*" I think to myself.

I look at the walls and the door. Something about the room feels familiar. I listen to hear if someone is in the home. Except for the birds and insects outside the window, everything is silent. I slowly twist the doorknob and open the door.

When I see the hallway, I know where I am. I fall to my knees and begin to cry. I am in my old home—the same home that lit up in flames the night the Patriots attacked us.

Our tiny two-bedroom apartment in the capital looks almost exactly the same. I press my face to the ground. I want to feel it against my skin, to know that it's real. After about five minutes, I stand up.

"If the house is here, maybe my family is too," a rush of excitement pulses through me.

I run from room to room, yelling for my mom, my dad, my little sister. No one replies. The house is empty.

Suddenly, the door creaks open, and a child runs into the room laughing. Then the little girl stops and looks at me in horror.

"Wh—who are you?" she stammers. "What are you doing in our house?"

I stare at the little girl in confusion.

"Uh, this is my house," I reply.

"You must be confused. You should leave. My mom is going to be home any minute now, and she will call the police," the girl says with a look of intensity in her eyes.

Her body remains in a stance that indicates she is ready to take off running at any moment.

I look around. There are many things about the place I don't recognize. The furniture is different. I start to doubt this is my home until I see a photo of my great-grandmother hanging on the wall to my right.

It's a Howard University graduation photo. From there, she also went to Columbia University in

New York to get a Ph.D. in education. But she prided herself on her roots, and so did the rest of the family, choosing to hang her Howard University graduation photo.

Her graduation cap is inconspicuously pinned to her cute little afro in the photo. She smiles with all her teeth and holds the rolled diploma in her hands so it fits within the frame.

"This is my home," I say, stepping toward the photo.

The girl takes three steps back, almost tripping over the carpet as soon as I start moving.

"That's my great-grandmother," I say.

"What are you talking about?" says the girl, completely confused and looking at me as if I'm crazy. "That's my mom!"

The words shake me.

"Where the fuck am I?" I think.

I look back at the girl and study her face intensely. Then I remember that none of this is real. I'm in a simulation. This is part of the test. I can tell she is getting scared and is about to start running.

"Look, I'm not going to hurt you, but what is your name?" I ask.

"Eliza," she says.

"My grandmother's younger sister's name," I think. *"Did this simulation recreate a time from the past before I was born? Why?"*

"What year is it?" I ask Eliza.

"Are you crazy?" she replies with a confused look on her face. "It's 1971, but you better get going. My mom will be here soon."

"1971," I repeat, mulling over the thought. "Did the simulation take me back in time? Why am I here? Why this year?"

"I don't know, but you better get going," Eliza insists.

"Look, I want to get going, but I don't know where to go," I reply.

Suddenly, it occurs to me that the girl may be warning me about wasting too much time in my home. This is a test, and I'm supposed to find the truth in a world full of lies.

"This photo," I turn back toward my great-grandmother's photo. "It's wrong. My great-grandmother didn't go to Howard. She went to the University of the District of Columbia. She always said she wanted to go to Howard but couldn't afford it."

"And you," I turn to the girl, who jumps back at the sudden rise in my voice. "You can't be Eliza. Eliza died at birth."

I start pacing back and forth. The girl begins to cry. At first, my emotions make it hard for me to see the truth, but now I understand that things around me aren't in their true form.

"*So, what is true?*" I think. I look around the room. Two newspapers lay open on the coffee table.

I pick up one of the papers. It's *The Washington Post*. I can't believe I'm actually holding a copy of the paper. After the crash, the staff at the paper refused to refocus on gathering business intelligence, and the billionaire running it chose to shut it down.

A slight sense of disappointment washes over me as I remember that I'm in a simulation and this isn't the actual paper. Though it's still amazing to see.

"It looks so real," I say out loud.

On the front cover, there is a story about former President Richard Nixon's new war on drugs.

"Get out of the house with your hands up," says a voice talking into a loudspeaker.

I suddenly look up. There are flashing red lights. The front door is open, and the girl is gone.

"*Shit,*" I think.

"Do as we say, and no one gets hurt," says the voice, clearly a police officer.

"*I don't have time for jail,*" I think.

I drop the paper and begin to run toward the back door. I hear footsteps running into the house. I don't look back. I quickly unlock and open the back door and dash down the stairs on the fire escape. As I'm running down the escape, I hear a voice.

"Don't move, or I'll shoot," says the voice.

I freeze. From the corner of my eye, I see him aiming his gun at me from the ground. I look up.

Cops are charging down the steps. My heart races as I search for an escape.

"Put your hands in the air," the cop on the ground yells.

I raise my hands. I'm out of ideas.

Several officers rush down the stairs after me. One grabs my left arm and shoves my body against the rusted metal on the fire escape. Another grabs my other arm and twists it behind my back so I can be handcuffed.

"Ahhh!" I scream in pain.

"Shut up!" the officer yells into my face. "I bet you're one of those drug users we're supposed to be after. Well, it's time to clean up the streets."

Both officers wrestle me to the floor of the fire escape. I yell out in pain again. They ignore me as they handcuff my arms. Then they pick me up and lead me down the fire escape.

As soon as I get to the ground, I kick the officer holding me in the groin and start to run until I hear the sound of a trigger being cocked.

"One more step, and I'll shoot," says the officer who had been on the ground waiting for me. "And trust me, with all this talk of drugs on the streets, no one will miss your Black ass."

I freeze, and my heart sinks. This simulation feels way too real. A mix of emotions—desperation, fear, and rage—washes over me.

"*It's 1971, alright,*" I think, mulling over the officer's words.

"That's a good girl," he says. "Now come on back here."

I slowly walk back toward the police. He opens the door to his car and shoves me in the back seat. Then he slams the door. I hear him talking to the other officers, but I can't make out his words. Then he gets into the car.

"Where are we going?" I ask.

"Where else? To jail, young lady. That's what happens when people break into homes," the officer replies.

"I don't have time for this, I..." my voice trails off.

"Yeah, I'm sure you have something really important to do," he says mockingly.

"Officer McNeary, you're needed as backup outside of the White House. Protests are getting out of hand," a voice says over the loudspeaker in the car.

"Copy," says the officer.

He starts the car. Then he turns on the overhead lights and sirens and begins maneuvering quickly through traffic.

I sit in the back seat in silence and despair, wondering how I'm going to win this round of tests if I'm stuck inside a jail cell within the simulation.

"*Why am I here?*" I think. "*Why this year?*"

I try to remember all the things my uncle taught me about the 1960s and 70s. Everything he told me about President Nixon.

"*Where can I find the truth here?*" I wonder.

I suddenly lose my train of thought. The police officer is swerving through the streets to get to this protest and almost hits a pedestrian. I let out a scream. He glances at me through his rearview mirror and chuckles.

My heart is pounding, and I want to cry. I know I'm still shaken up mentally from the first accident in the real world with the taxi driver.

As we approach the White House, I hear faint sounds of people chanting.

"Hell no, we won't go. Hell no, we won't go," they say.

Before we reach the White House, traffic slows to a standstill. I look out the window and see that the roads are completely blocked. Cars are jammed one behind the other, and people are standing outside their vehicles, trying to see what's causing the gridlock.

"Shit," says the officer. "Don't you move. I'm going in."

The officer grabs his walkie-talkie from the passenger seat and runs toward the chaos.

"What is going on?" I yell after him.

He ignores me and disappears into the crowd.

In the distance, I see a small group of young adults approaching the police car. One holds a sign that reads, *End the War Before It Ends You.*

"*Oh, they're protesting the Vietnam War,*" I think.

I remember my uncle telling me that this year is when discontent surrounding the war is at its peak. The war has been going on for years, and though government officials keep saying the United States is winning, there seems to be no end in sight.

The war in Vietnam began as a fight against the French for independence. After Ho Chi Minh, the Vietnamese leader at the time, didn't receive support from the U.S. for its fight against the French, he reached out to the Russians. They supplied him with weapons and communist ideology.

Communism is a political theory where the government controls the market by setting prices for wages and goods.

The United States entered the war in Vietnam after Ho Chi Minh adopted communism. U.S. leaders feared that if communism caught on in Vietnam, it would spread throughout the region. They hoped to contain the ideology.

Thousands of Americans died in the war, and after some time, the public began to question the cost. In 1969, Richard Nixon won the presidency campaigning on a promise to end the war, which had become a thorn in the side of former President Lyndon B. Johnson.

But when Nixon became president, he didn't end the war. Some said it was pride because it would be the first military defeat in U.S. history.

"Find the truth in the lies," I think.

When the group of young protesters reaches the car, one gets out a slim piece of steel and uses it to open the back door of the police car where I'm sitting.

"Be free, fellow resistor," he says.

I am in so much shock I don't know what to say. I immediately jump out of the car and start running in the same direction the police officer went.

As I approach the crowd, I smell tear gas. I start to gag and do my best to hold my breath. People who have been occupying the streets and camped in a nearby park are suddenly running, screaming, and coughing. Police in riot gear are arresting anyone they can catch.

The scene is chaotic. My eyes water, and I start coughing. I lift my shirt with my hands and use it to cover my nose and mouth. I have to squint intensely, barely able to see what's happening around me.

Suddenly, I see a man in riot gear heading in my direction. I start to run the other way, but he sets his sights on me and begins chasing me through the crowd.

"*I can't get arrested again,*" I think.

I feel for my pocket knife, wondering if it's still on me even though I'm in a simulation. My heart sinks. It's gone.

Just ahead of me, I see a sign attached to a stick lying on the ground. I dash for it. Then the officer pounces on my legs, knocking us both to the

121

ground. We struggle for a minute, each of us desperate to overtake the other.

I reach up and feel the tip of the stick with my fingers. I grab it and swing at the officer, knocking the gas mask off his face. He tries to stand and regain his composure, but I swing again, knocking his face to the side.

He stumbles and fumbles for his weapon. I panic, tackle him to the ground, take his weapon from the holster at his waist, and shoot him in the leg.

He yells out in anguish. But it's nothing compared to the chaos that erupts around me. Suddenly, I hear several gunshots and screams. Fearful police officers have opened fire on the protesters. No one can see clearly through the gas. I put on the officer's mask, tuck the gun into my waistband, and begin running away from the crowd.

"*This isn't how things happened,*" I think. "*There were Vietnam protesters shot, but that was at a university the year before. My actions must be messing with the simulation.*"

As I'm running, the sight of one guy makes me stop. He's the only person not running from the chaos. He's standing with a gas mask, frantically taking photos while people flee around him. A badge hangs around his neck with the word *PRESS* written in big letters.

"*Find the truth within the lies,*" I think, staring at him.

Then it dawns on me. This year, one of the biggest lies in the world is exposed by *The New York Times*, which publishes the Pentagon Papers. It's a series of documents showing how government officials lied to the American people about the status of the Vietnam War.

For years, intelligence officials knew they were losing the war and there was little hope of turning things around, but presidents kept raising the number of troops in the country, sharing false promises of hope for victory when there was none. That was the most important truth to be discovered this year.

"But they don't publish this article for several months," I think. *"I can't possibly go all the way to NYC and figure out what they're doing there!"*

I look around frantically, wondering if there's a bus I can take to New York. Cops are arresting people all around me and closing in. I start to run.

"I need to get as far away from this mess as possible," I think.

As I glance around, I see a male protester stumbling and coughing, trying to run through the smoke but struggling. Police are closing in on him. Instinctively, I grab his hand.

"Follow me," I tell him.

He clutches my hand and runs behind me as I guide him through the chaos. It's easier for me to see with the gas mask, and I figure the least I can do is help someone else.

"Where are you going?" he asks breathlessly.

"Anywhere but here," I yell back.

We run through streets and alleyways until the sound of police sirens becomes distant, and we can no longer breathe from exertion.

"T-thank you," he stammers.

I lean against a wall, take off the gas mask, and slide to the ground, breathless. I can't respond for several seconds.

"I—I need to find a bus to New York City," I finally say.

"Who are you?" His eyes scan my attire, then rest on the gun tucked into my waistband.

"I'm not going to hurt you," I reply. "I just saved you. I just need to know where the bus is."

He studies me carefully. He's young and pale, with blonde wavy hair that stops just above his shoulders. He wears blue jeans, a white shirt, and a black backpack slung over his shoulder. His deep blue eyes narrow as he squints at me.

"Why do you want to go to New York?" he asks. "The resistance is here."

"Look, I didn't ask for your opinion on my trip to New York City. I just need to know how to get there," I snap.

He looks taken aback by my tone. I remember that 1971 isn't exactly the height of equality. He probably isn't used to women—especially Black women—speaking to him that way.

"You'll need to catch a train from Union Station," he explains. "I'm heading back to the protest area."

"Why would you do that?" I ask. "You'll get arrested!"

"Either way, I get arrested," he says, pulling a paper from his bag and waving it in front of me. Several other papers fall to the ground.

It's a draft card with the name *Charlie McDaniels* written on it. My heart sinks a little. I understand now. If he dodges the Vietnam War draft, he's going to jail. He stuffs the card back into his bag and kneels to pick up the papers that fell.

"I plan to join a group burning these cards later tonight," he says.

"I understand," I reply, kneeling to help him gather the papers.

As I collect them, one brochure catches my eye. It has a purple logo with the letters *R-A-N-D* in bold at the top.

"RAND," I say aloud, holding the paper and staring at it.

"*Something about this,*" I think. "*Something about this company is important.*"

I close my eyes, trying to remember.

"What did my uncle say about this company?"

"What are you doing?" Charlie asks, taking the paper from my hand.

"RAND!" I exclaim. "What do you know about it?"

"It's one of the top think tanks in Washington, D.C.—if not the nation. I have an interview for an internship there next week," he replies. "Getting that internship would be a dream come true."

I look at him intently, feeling a surge of clarity. This kid is giving me a clue. He's a clue built into the simulation.

"How do I get to RAND?" I ask.

"You're not going to New York City anymore?" he asks, raising an eyebrow. "Why do you want to go to RAND now?"

"I just need to check something," I reply.

"They'll never let you in without an appointment," he says, shaking his head. "That place is top secret."

"Look, I don't have time for debate! Just tell me where it is!" My voice rises with urgency.

He takes two steps back, raising his hands.

"Relax, okay. You can take the RS bus on Constitution Avenue and 14th Street. It'll take you down to Pentagon City. You can't miss it."

I immediately start running toward Constitution Avenue.

"Thank you!" I yell over my shoulder.

"Bye!" he calls back.

I'm not sure what I'll find at RAND, but something deep in my memory—maybe something my uncle once said—tells me I need to be there.

By the time I reach Constitution Avenue and 14th Street, I'm breathless. I lean against the bus stop sign and catch my breath. Almost immediately, the RS bus pulls up in front of me, and I hop on.

The young man was right. I know when we're approaching the RAND building. It's large, with a purple sign displaying the letters *R-A-N-D* in bold white font.

The bus stops across the street from the building. I hop off and turn toward it. A security guard in a white uniform stands at the front door. Each person entering the building shows a badge before the guard motions for them to pass.

I have no plan as I approach the door.

"*Look like you belong here,*" I think to myself as I get closer.

"Whoa, whoa, whoa! Slow down, young lady," the guard says, stretching out his hand to stop me. "What brings you here? Do you have an appointment?"

"Uh, I—I'm here to interview for an internship," I reply.

"Are you on the schedule? What's your name?" he asks, pulling out a schedule book from under a desk.

"Charlie McDaniels," I reply.

I can tell he's about to tell me I'm not on the list. His eyes scan the page, and his head begins to lift.

"My interview was originally scheduled for next week, but someone called me this morning to tell me it was rescheduled for today," I say quickly.

His face is stern as he flips the page, scanning with his eyes. Then, his expression softens slightly as his eyes land on the name *Charlie McDaniels*.

"Go on in. The receptionist at the front desk will call the person you're supposed to meet," he says, gesturing for me to move past him.

I walk in toward the receptionist's desk, but as soon as the security guard turns back to his post, I walk briskly past the desk without making eye contact and turn left down a long hallway.

A group of people wearing suits and holding notebooks exits a room. It looks like a meeting just ended. One man walks past me and glances back suspiciously. I avoid making eye contact and keep walking.

I know I can't sneak around for long. There can't be that many Black people at RAND in the 1970s. I start looking frantically for clues. Signs on the doors read things like *Education Studies* and *Population and Migration*.

Suddenly, I notice the man who looked at me suspiciously speaking to a security officer and pointing in my direction.

I walk faster and turn another corner. Glancing back to see if I'm being followed, I bump into someone and fall to the ground. His notebook and papers scatter around us.

"Are you alright, young lady?" the older man asks. He's in his late thirties or early forties, with thick black-and-gray hair that curls slightly at the ends.

He stretches out his hand to help me up. I catch a glimpse of his badge: *Daniel Ellsberg*.

"Stop!" I hear the security guard running down the hallway toward me.

I push Daniel's hand aside, scramble to my feet, and start running again. My eyes dart around as I sprint. A few feet ahead, I see a door with the word *Vietnam* written on it.

I dash toward it.

"Stop! Stop, or I'll shoot!" the guard shouts.

I freeze.

"*Could I die in a simulation?*" I wonder.

"Hands in the air! Now!" the guard yells.

I think back to the waiver I signed.

"*I might be able to die,*" I conclude.

I'm almost certain the answers I need are just beyond that door. But I don't want to risk being arrested again—not when I'm this close.

"I—I got lost," I stammer. "I don't want any trouble. I just got lost and was looking for a way out."

"Hands up and face on the ground," the guard says.

"Is that really necess—" I start.

"I said hands up and face on the ground!" he yells.

With every second that passes, I become more aware of the racial dynamics at play. At this point, several people have stepped into the hallway to see what's happening.

"*I could fight,*" I think. "*I have a gun. But this could end poorly.*"

I slowly raise my hands and drop to my knees.

"I said face to the ground," the guard barks.

"Is that really necessary?" I shout back, feeling my blood boil.

"This isn't real," I remind myself. "It's just a simulation."

I hear the click of his gun being cocked. The whispers in the hallway fall silent.

"I said face," the guard pauses and lowers his voice, "to the ground."

I take a deep breath and wonder how the simulation would react if I pulled out my gun and shot him. Then I remember Emre, my family, and Station 7. My mission is bigger than my ego.

I put my face to the cold, hard floor.

The officer rushes toward me, grabs my hands, and locks them in handcuffs.

"Let me help you find your way out of here," he says, lifting me to my feet and holding me by the wrist.

He walks me to the exit, uncuffs me, and shoves me outside.

"Get on now! Before I have you arrested," he says.

I glare at him but walk across the street to the bus stop and sit on the bench. My heart is racing. I'm angry, humiliated, and disappointed.

"I was so close," I think. *"How am I going to get back in there now?"*

I stare at the building across the street. Despite my rage, I can't help but be momentarily distracted by how beautiful the simulation world is.

The sun is setting behind the building, illuminating the sky with pink, purple, and orange streaks. I know it's fake, but I can't help but appreciate its beauty and the warmth around me.

I think back to the real world, where it's winter most of the year. Beautiful spring days like this don't exist anymore.

I watch people get on and off the buses that stop in front of me. They don't seem to notice the warmth or the beautiful sunset. They don't appreciate it.

"How could they know this would all soon be gone? How could they know the planet was already responding to the havoc they were wreaking on it?" I wonder.

I know I'm supposed to be on a mission, and there are horrible things about this time period. But at least these people have spring. I sit completely distracted from my mission, marveling at the warmth and sunset. Then I lie down on the bench, close my eyes, and decide to enjoy it.

When I open my eyes again, it's pitch dark. I must have fallen asleep. I scurry to my feet and feel around my body to make sure my gun is still on me. It's still tucked into my waistband under my shirt. I let out a sigh of relief and turn toward the RAND building.

The building appears empty, and everything around it is dark except for one streetlight.

Then, to my surprise, the door of the building opens, and a man steps out. His head turns from side to side, as if he's checking to make sure no one sees him. He's carrying a briefcase clutched close to his body. He locks the door and starts walking toward me—or better yet, toward the bus stop.

As he approaches, I realize it's the man I bumped into earlier: Daniel Ellsberg. I turn away, partially covering my face, hoping he won't recognize me. He stands next to me at the bus stop, looking anxious. He holds his briefcase tight and repeatedly glances at his watch.

Finally, the bus arrives, and he gets on. I hurriedly follow him and sit a few rows behind. He rests the briefcase on his lap, gripping it tightly. My mind races as I try to come up with a plan.

"What could I say to him?" I think. *"Should I tell him I need help getting into the RAND building? Why would he help me? Why would he even talk to me?"*

"Next stop, please," Daniel says to the driver.

I look around and notice how old the buses are. There are no levers or strings to pull to signal a stop. Passengers have to speak to the driver.

I stand and walk toward the door, hoping Daniel won't notice me if I get off first. Maybe it's just a coincidence that we're both at the same stop—the only two on the bus—getting off at the same place.

The bus stops. I get off and start walking to the right. Daniel gets off as well and also turns right. I keep walking, listening carefully to make sure his footsteps are still behind me.

Then he turns right again toward a strip mall. Out of the corner of my eye, I see him enter what appears to be a closed store with the word *Advertising* on the front.

I turn and walk after him. When I reach the door, I press my ear against it, trying to hear what's inside. It's silent. I twist the knob, and to my relief, it creaks open.

I step inside and close the door behind me. The place is completely dark. I move deeper into the store, keeping my steps as light as possible and feeling along the walls to guide my path.

I hear a faint sound in the distance—something like a machine blowing air. I follow the sound into the darkness.

As I get closer, I see a faint, white fluorescent light ahead. Then I hear someone breathing and rustling papers.

Suddenly, the sound stops.

"Is anyone out there?" the voice calls out.

I freeze.

I haven't thought about how I would approach this person, but with time ticking, there's no moment to plan.

"Raise your hands and step away from the machine, or I'll shoot," I say to the man.

He freezes and begins shaking. Slowly, he lifts his hands and steps away from the machine. I can see now that it's Daniel. The briefcase lies open on the ground next to the copy machine, and he's been copying whatever documents are inside.

"If you want to arrest me, go ahead," Daniel says. "But these documents need to reach the world. This war could come to a nuclear end, killing hundreds of millions of people. We've lost thousands of brave men and women to a war that should have never happened."

I glance at one of the papers that drops from his hand to the floor. It has the words *TOP SECRET* in bold letters stamped on the top and bottom of the document.

Details from my uncle's lessons rush back into my memory. I realize what I've walked into.

"This man is the leaker!" I think with excitement.

Daniel Ellsberg is a military analyst with top security clearance. He helped draft the Pentagon Papers, a study of U.S. government decision-making in relation to the Vietnam War. While working at the RAND Corporation, he copied and leaked thousands of pages of the document to *The New York Times*.

His research showed that the U.S. stood little chance of winning the war without nuclear fallout. When he learned that nuclear options were on the table and millions of lives were at risk, he decided to leak the documents in hopes of bringing public accountability to the war.

In response, President Nixon made a series of poor decisions to control leaks. Some of the things he instructed his staff to do were illegal. Eventually, they were caught and arrested, and Nixon was forced to resign.

I am smitten by the papers. I drop my gun, pick up a stack of documents from his briefcase, and hold them in my hands.

"This is it," I think. *"This is the truth in a world full of lies."*

I look at Daniel, who stares back at me in confusion and disbelief. It's been a long time since I've seen someone act with so much integrity. It's been a long time since I've seen anyone use information to help people instead of manipulate and control them. It's been a long time since I lived in a free and functioning democratic society.

In the real world, there are no more Ellsbergs—or, if there are, there's no one left to leak to.

This moment, in this dark room, feels beautiful. It's something the real world no longer has, and suddenly, I don't want to go back.

I hold the top-secret documents—what will later be known as the Pentagon Papers—close to my chest and cry.

Then, the white fluorescent light from the copy machine fills the room, and all I can see is white.

9

Winner Takes All

"Congratulations," I hear a muffled voice say.

I feel something being removed from my face. I open my eyes, but the world is a blur. I rub my eyes in an effort to focus on the blurred figures in front of me.

"I can't believe you're only the second person out, and it's been a week!" the same voice exclaims.

When my eyes come back into focus, I see it's the exotic woman from Station 7. A pang of sadness hits me as I realize I'm no longer in the simulation. I'm back in the station.

"Only the second person?" I mumble.

"Well, yes, which is great for you because that means you won't have much competition during the final test," she replies.

As things become clearer, I realize I'm still sitting in the big chair I climbed into a while ago. My hands are free, and the simulation helmet is gone.

Suddenly, I remember who my competition is.

"*Emre!*" I think to myself.

I turn to my right and see him still in the simulation. His hands are cuffed to the armrest, and his fists are clenched. I can tell that wherever he is in the simulation, he isn't happy. Sadness stirs inside me.

"*I wish I could help him,*" I think.

"Why the sad look on your face? You should be excited," says the redhead.

I turn toward her and begin processing the words she just said.

"What do you mean it's already been a week?" I exclaim.

"Oh, I forgot to mention to you all. Time seems shorter within the simulation, so a day in there is actually a week in the real world," she replies.

"What? How could you forget to say that?" I ask in disbelief.

She shrugs.

"It seems like you're all making it out okay," she replies. "Just be glad you've made it this far and prepare for the next test. That one's going to be a doozy."

I stare at her in shock. Something about her expression seems strange, almost like she's really happy to see that I made it. But why would she be happy to see me? She looks at me again, as if she wants to say something else, then turns and walks away.

I push myself out of the chair and walk around, checking how many of the people I've come to view as friends are still in the simulation. Everyone except for James is still there.

My heart sinks, and my mind races. What box did they tick on the waiver we signed? Death after two weeks or risk taking off the helmet and going mad? Is there any way I can help them? I wish I could tell them to hurry up. There must be a way to communicate.

The redhead pokes her head back into the door.

"Uhhh, you can't stay in here," she says. "We can't risk anything happening to the people in the simulation. You should gather your things. Dinner will be served in the common area. Then you'll want to get some sleep. You're lucky—we're giving you all a week to recover before the next assignment. For those who make it out at the last minute, that won't be enough recovery time."

I glance at her, then back at Emre and the others. I still wonder how I can help them. The redhead clears her throat, snapping me out of my trance. I slowly gather my bag and walk out of the room behind her. A guard closes the door behind me, and my heart sinks at the thud.

As we walk down the hallway, I feel as if my head is in a trance. It's almost like I'm still in the simulation.

"Dinner will be served in here today," says the exotic woman, gesturing toward a room.

"You should get some real food. It'll help you rebuild strength so you're ready for the next test," she continues.

When the scent of baked bread hits my nose, my body pings with hunger. I hadn't realized how weak and hungry I was. My legs march toward the smell, as if I no longer control them.

It always amazes me how so many things in our society have changed, but the dining hall still resembles a public school cafeteria. Ten long white tables stretch across the room, with benches attached to either side so people can sit across from each other. The setup makes it easy to enter and exit without bothering others.

Along one wall is a bar of warm food, and a smaller cold food bar with a drink station sits adjacent to it. Cooks stand behind the warm food bar, ready to serve people as they arrive with empty trays.

I pick up a tray and grab two hot rolls, quickly eating one in hopes no one notices my greed. The sweet, warm, buttery taste fills me with an unexplainable feeling of gratitude toward Station 7. The place isn't perfect, but it's hard to imagine life outside these walls, where I'd have to fight every day for bread this fresh.

Normally, food is rationed at each meal, but I figure since I might have missed a few meals in the simulation, I'll grant myself a pass.

I move to the woman serving macaroni and cheese that stretches in long, gooey strings. She gives me an intense look, as if she knows I took an extra roll. But when I point to the macaroni, she simply smiles and serves me. This continues until my tray is full.

Turning toward the cafeteria, I get a feeling that reminds me of junior high school. Since the test began, I've sat with my co-competitors—people who've become the closest thing I've had to friends in years. I mean, I treated them like friends. They were my friends. Now I'm alone in a sea of strangers.

The idea of making small talk with strangers when I have so much on my mind seems ridiculous. I scan the room for an empty table. Then I see James. He's hunched over his food, seemingly avoiding small talk too. I remember him being relatively social in the past. Maybe the tests have changed him. I place my tray beside his.

"So you made it," he says without looking up.

"I'm here. I'm alive," I reply, sitting down beside him and starting to eat.

"If you eat too fast, it'll make you sick," he says, peering at me from the corner of his eye. "I say that because I got sick."

I suddenly realize I haven't been chewing between bites. I decide to follow his advice.

"When did you get out?" I ask, my mouth half full.

"Two days ago," he replies.

"I was hoping I'd be the only one," he adds with a smirk.

"How could you say that?" I glare at him, remembering the others stuck in the simulation and the paper we all signed granting us possible madness or death if we didn't get out.

"Let's be clear," James says, looking at me directly. "There may be moments when we act like allies or friends to get to the next round, but no one here is anyone's ally or friend. Only one person can win."

I shake my head at James and decide to focus on my food.

"What? You seriously think your guy Emre is any different?" James says with a look mixed with pity and disgust. "I'd be really careful about that guy if I were you. You may not ask around, but I do, and rumor has it that every time he gets close to a partner during these competitions, they disappear."

When he says it, my throat clamps up. The food I was enjoying suddenly turns sour, and my stomach churns. I think about the girl Emre told me disappeared. Could it be possible that he only told me part of the story?

"Wh-what do you mean?" I ask, hating myself for stammering, for visibly losing confidence.

"Exactly what I said, Feonix," James replies. "Look, it's no benefit to me to tell you this. I don't care if you disappear or not—that's one less person I'm competing with. But watching you think you have friends or allies in this place? It's pathetic."

My body goes cold. I can't hide the shiver that runs down my spine. A feeling I haven't felt in a long time—sadness and betrayal—sweeps over me.

I glance at James. There isn't an ounce of remorse in his expression. I can't help but wonder how he operates with such callousness, without a care for anyone around him.

"Why?" I ask. "Why are you in this competition?"

"I don't think you've fully taken in the stakes of this competition, Feonix," he says, his tone condescending.

I feel my anger rising. I'm angry at the world, but I tell myself I won't lose control again.

"Answer the question, James," I reply.

"In this world, we have nothing—no money, no power," he says, staring directly at me now. "We stopped living a long time ago. We simply survive. People, particularly my people, have little to look forward to in a world pervaded by ignorance. But this is a chance to turn things around, to run the most influential organization in the world. Don't you get it, Feonix? Winner takes all!"

There's a fire behind his eyes, almost a bit of madness. He's right—I haven't taken in all the stakes of this competition. I've just been trying to survive, moving with little to no purpose. It's all too much to take in. I can't even finish my food.

"Why are you in this competition?" James snaps at me.

I can't answer him. I think about Emre's mission and my promise to my uncle. I realize I'm no longer certain about what's driving me. I pick up my tray of food and start to walk away.

"That's what I thought," James calls after me. "I plan to win!"

I keep walking. I don't stop until I reach my room and lock the door behind me. I place the tray on my bed and try to hold back the tears, but they fall anyway. Soon, I'm lying on my bed, weeping. I haven't felt so alone since the day my uncle died.

"*How many partners did Emre actually have?*" I wonder. "*Did they really all disappear? Maybe James is lying to tear us apart? He seemed a little jealous.*"

James plans to take over this entity and all the people who follow it. He doesn't care who falls around him. I don't even think he cares about the truth. He just wants power.

I'm tired. I'm tired of being surrounded by people with dubious ambitions. I'm tired of living in a world where everyone seems to climb over each other to reach the top, taking whatever scraps are left. Like crabs in a boiling pot.

At that moment, I selfishly wonder why I survived when our home was burned to the ground by the Patriots, why I survived when violence swept through our city following the news director's announcement of her illness, why I survived when my taxi spun out of control during the first test, and why I'm here now, alive. I don't want to be here, in this world, alone. I don't know who or what I'm living for.

That night, I cry until I fall asleep.

I wake up just before dawn and decide to leave the station. I grab the keys to Emre's car from my desk, a jacket, and a new backpack. Then I exit the room and Station 7.

As I start to drive, I'm not quite sure where I'm going. But in the middle of the drive, I know.

I pull up in front of the old, shoddy apartment building. The car looks so out of place in this neighborhood. It's not new, but it isn't as old and rusted as everything else. The brick building has a rusted-out fire escape and multiple broken windows. Weeds, glass from shattered beer bottles, and other trash litter the overgrown lawn.

I get out of the car and look around. It's as if the place has been abandoned. I walk with some trepidation to the back of the building. On the way, I pluck dried blades of grass—the closest thing to flowers I can find. This neighborhood, my old neighborhood, has been overtaken by violence and gang activity since I left. Everyone knows it's no

145

longer safe. I instinctively feel for my knives and panic when I realize I forgot to bring them.

I'm not sure I'll find what I'm looking for since so many years have passed. But then I see it, and tears well in my eyes. My uncle's grave, with the same marker I made for him. I'm surprised to see that the grass around his grave is maintained and that other graves have been erected around his own. I slowly approach it and lay the bouquet of weeds and grass on top.

"I'm sorry," I tell him. "I don't think I can keep my promise. I tried. I really tried."

Tears stream down my face.

"I feel so alone here. So alone in this world." I lift my head to the sky, even though I don't believe in Heaven or Hell. "Why am I here alone?"

"I know you," says a voice behind me.

My body jolts in fear. I hadn't heard anyone approaching. I stumble back and use my hands to crawl away from the voice.

"Relax," the man says, stooping down and reaching out a hand to help me up. "I'm not going to hurt you."

I look up at the man. His hair is almost completely gray. He's pale and wears a faded black jacket over worn blue-jean overalls and brown rubber boots. Beside him is a red bucket with a large pair of rusting scissors inside.

"Because of you, I find fulfillment in maintaining this space," he says, extending his hand closer.

Still shaking from the shock and now the cold, I take his hand. He helps me up.

"We're all proud of you, and your uncle would be too," he says. "Not many people make it out of these parts alive. But you did, and you're at Station 7. We're rooting for you to take it over."

"How do you know me?" I ask.

"Well, to be honest, we've never met," he replies, shifting his feet along the ground. "But we're a small community."

He gestures toward the building.

"We've all heard your story—received hope from your story. That's why I volunteered to maintain the graves. Honoring you as the living and your family as the dead," he explains.

"No one from our community has done what you've done. And we know no one has won the contest yet, but boy, are we rooting for you," he continues.

"You must be mist-mistaken," I choke out.

"I can't believe it's you!" says a voice from behind the man.

A teenage girl steps out from her hiding spot behind a tree and begins to approach us. She's clearly still in her pajamas and barefoot.

"Zenya, you shouldn't be here," the old man says. "It's not safe."

"My mom was watching you through the window, but I had to see you for myself!" She runs toward me now. "I can't believe it's really you! What are you doing here? Shouldn't you be taking over Station 7?"

Her arms fling around me in a hug. I step back in instinctive defense, then slowly lower my hands to pat her back. Then she starts crying.

"I—I used to doubt the stories," she says through muffled tears. "That you would take over and bring the light, the truth, but now I finally see you!"

I'm stunned.

"I—I can't d—" I start.

"The world needs truth and healing," the old man interrupts. "We don't need another selfish ruler trying to co-opt resources and power. The truth is the sting, but only after it's revealed can we begin to pick up the pieces. Before the crash, we lived in a society where we appreciated the messiness of truth. And we believe you have what it takes to take over and restore it."

I look up at the building and see faces peering down at us through some of the windows. In one window, a child smiles and waves as we lock eyes.

"You are where you are for a reason, Feonix," the old man continues. "Many have applied and haven't even gotten past the first step. Zenya and many others are depending on you. You must understand that you're not only in this for yourself."

I wave at the child, then crouch down to make eye contact with the girl hugging me.

"To tell you the truth, I came here today to quit," I say, glancing up at the old man.

"No!" says the girl.

"I know," the old man replies. "I overheard."

Zenya starts to cry—this time tears of sadness. I cup her hands in my own to try to comfort her.

"It's just... I feel like I lost my sense of why I'm doing all this," I continue. "I've been thinking so selfishly this whole time. I thought I was doing this to fulfill a promise to myself and my uncle. The stakes are so high—the freedom of every person in the country depends on who wins. But I don't know if I'm the one who can take over and run things the right way."

"Do you believe in standing for truth and fighting against those who lie for their own power?" asks the man.

"That's all I've wanted to do since the day I lost my family," I reply.

"In the fire," the man says, looking down at the ground.

"Yes," I choke out.

"Look, it brings me no pleasure to reveal this to you, but part of the reason I'm here is to honor you, and the other part is penance," he says.

He shifts back and forth as if he has an itch on the bottom of his foot that moving could relieve.

"I used to be a Patriot," he says.

At those words, my heart freezes, and my stomach churns at the same time. I don't want to hear what he has to say next, but I can't stop listening.

"In fact, my brother used to be a faction leader," he continues. "And I believed, deeply, that people like you and Zenya were evil. I helped attack this community that night when all hell broke loose."

Tears I can't stop begin to stream down my face. I quiver as I hold on to Zenya.

"But later on, my brother revealed to me that his motives for attacking the faction were based on lies," he says.

I freeze at those words. Goosebumps cover my body.

"What do you mean?" I reply.

"You see, originally, they believed the faction leader worked with the Chinese to keep us poor. They had, quote, insider information from a woman named Kathryn Richards. A beautiful young girl with reddish-brown curls and caramel skin. I don't know who she worked for. I always thought she was from one of the federal intelligence agencies. Anyway, it was believed whoever she worked for wanted favors from the head of Latus—your father—that he wasn't willing to give, so they used us to remove him. When my brother learned the truth, he didn't care. He felt Latus had it coming anyway. But I was haunted by what I did. I eventually left the faction and joined

Latus. I've dedicated my life to helping my new faction and atoning for my past."

I look at the old man. He's one of the people who killed my family. He took everything I had. And yet, I can't bring myself to hate him. The look of hurt on his face tells me he expects me to react negatively to this information.

I look back down at the little girl in my arms, then up at all the people in the windows. I have thousands of social followers, but these people in my old neighborhood feel more real to me than any of them. It makes me feel less alone and a little ashamed.

Deception is my enemy, I conclude in my mind—not this man or the other Patriots. It's the use of disinformation to deceive, control, and manipulate people that got my family killed, and the people who are willing to do such things.

With the privilege of my position, how can I just give up? Some of these children will only know war and strife because of the persistent onslaught of disinformation that keeps our nation consistently unstable. At that moment, I realize I have many reasons to be the one who takes over Station 7.

I look back at the man.

"I forgive you. You don't need to seek atonement from me," I say. "In fact, now, I really understand why I need to do this. And that's thanks, in part, to you."

I nod at the old man. He smiles.

"Does—does that mean you won't give up?" asks the girl, lifting her hands to wipe her tears.

"It means I'm going to keep trying," I reply.

When Zenya lifts her hands to wipe her tears, I notice the bracelet on her wrist. The symbol on it looks familiar, but I can't remember where I've seen it before.

"Where did you get this bracelet?" I ask.

"President Rivers," she replies.

The old man lets out a big sigh. A look of disgust creeps over his face.

"They've been going through all the poor neighborhoods, testing the youth, recruiting—sometimes by force—the ones with high scores. Rumor has it that Rivers is trying to build an army and wants to take over Station 7 in the process. She wants to eliminate the factions and concentrate power in the center. She's been preaching that it's the only way to effectively combat foreign threats," the old man says. "Anyone who's already been tested has to wear the symbol. It's their sign of loyalty to the government."

I pull the girl's arm closer and inspect the symbol—a blue wedged cross surrounded by a circle made of leaves.

"I've seen this before," I mutter.

"They're everywhere," says the girl.

Then the image flashes in my mind again—the tattoo on Emre's inner thigh. He has the same symbol. My heart sinks.

"I have to go," I say, looking between the both of them.

"Was it something I said?" asks the old man.

"No," I reply, running toward the car. "I need to get back to the mission."

"Good luck!" he yells after me.

Questions flood my mind as I drive back toward the station.

"Could Emre be working for President Rivers?"

I realize it's a miracle I've made it this far in the competition. I've constantly been two steps behind, missing the bigger picture.

"*Not anymore,*" I think to myself. "*I owe it to these people, to my uncle, my parents, my sister, and myself to finish this. But first, I need to help those stuck in the simulation.*"

I decide that if I'm going to be the winner who takes it all, I need to know Station 7 and everyone in it better. I need to take control beyond the test. I need a plan. I also need allies. It's time to be on the offensive.

PART TWO
THE TRUTH

10

Dangerous Liaisons

When I return to the station, I go straight to my room. I want to gather supplies and make a plan.

But when I open the door, Emre is sitting on my bed. A look of delight and excitement sweeps over his face when he sees me.

I am horrified.

After we stand staring with opposite expressions for about 15 seconds, his smile fades, and I can tell he knows I know.

"You don't look so happy to see me," he says, adjusting his position.

"Don't move, or I'll kill you," I say, quickly picking up a knife from my desk.

He lifts both hands as an indication of innocence.

"I said, don't move!" I scream.

"Look, I don't know what people have told you, but I don't plan to hurt you," he says.

"Why should I believe anything you say?" I yell at him. "Who the fuck are you?"

"You know who I am," he yells back. "I haven't been dishon—"

"Oh, but you haven't told me everything either," I interject. "What exactly does that tattoo on your thigh mean, Emre? Where are your previous competition partners?"

Emre dives for his backpack.

I throw my knife, aiming for his chest. It grazes his shoulder. He grabs my ankle and pulls me to the ground. My head hits the floor with a loud thud. I try to roll onto my back and regain my stance, but Emre maintains his grip on my leg, dragging me across the floor.

I sit up and punch him across the face, causing him to loosen his grip. I quickly but clumsily climb back onto my feet.

"I don't want to hurt you," Emre says.

"What happened to your other partners?" I ask again.

We are both on our feet now. I stand on one side of the room, and he stands on the other. I embrace an attack stance I don't fully feel comfortable in and glance between him and the objects I could use to defend myself if he charges. I wish I were close enough to my closet to grab another knife, but they're out of reach, and I don't want Emre to notice them.

"I have a mission to complete. Everything I told you about what Station 7 has done is true. And it's my goal to put an end to the falsehoods and lies that drive our country into factions, making us weak and vulnerable. Station 7 grows more powerful while we, as a nation, grow more divided. The United States was once a single nation—the most powerful in the world. I've committed my life to restoring that," Emre says.

"And the partn—" I start again.

"This mission is bigger than any one person," Emre interjects.

He uses his right arm to throw his backpack at my face. I dodge it, but then I feel the back of his heel against my ribcage. I reach for the hairdryer he used to fix my hair not too long ago and whack him across the face as he charges me.

The pang of pain from his kick to my ribcage makes me fall to my knees, holding my side. Emre knocks me to the ground and cups my throat with both hands. The right side of his face is bruised and bloodied.

"I didn't want it to come to this," Emre says. "But this mission is bigger than you and me."

At that moment, I know he killed them. My heart breaks. The rush of emotions blurs my thinking and vision.

Emre tightens his grip on my throat. I know he's going to kill me. I reach around the room for any object to get him off me—anything I can hit him with. I am losing air. In fear and panic, I dig my nails into his wrist, hoping it will force him to loosen his grip, but he only presses down harder. I gasp, but no air comes into my lungs. Tears stream down my face.

"You were so smart. You saw things, caught mistakes other editors would let slip. You questioned everything. That's why I chose to work with you. And you really are beautiful," his words are haunting.

The world around me begins to turn gray as if the color is being sucked out of it. I always imagine myself having profound thoughts at this moment, knowing I'm going to die. I think of the girl, Zenya. My heart sinks, knowing there's no hope for her, the old man, or the child in the window.

I think of the people I want to help still in the simulation—Ray, Titan, Alex, and even Gabby. They're out of my reach. I can't even save myself. What will the world look like once I'm gone and Emre or James takes over Station 7?

Suddenly, the door swings open, and I hear several footsteps storm into the room. One person in a white security force uniform knocks Emre off me and onto the ground.

I pop up and take multiple gasps for air. From the corner of my eye, I see two security figures holding him down while another puts him in handcuffs. I try to get up, but my body is in shock.

I feel hands grab my limbs and turn my face to the ground. Cold metal handcuffs trap my wrists behind my back. I'm still struggling to catch my breath, but I can't. Then everything goes dark.

I wake up in fear and panic. I struggle to get out of the glass pod-like container, but my body is strapped down.

"She's awake," I hear a voice say.

"Great, then transfer her to the holding cells for prisoners," a second voice says.

As my pod opens, several security force members surround me. They unlatch my arms and legs and lift my body. They keep a tight grip on my limbs, so even though I struggle, I can't escape. Then they cuff my arms behind my back and place my bare feet on the cold ground.

"Walk," one security force member says, shoving me in the back.

As I begin to walk, I realize I recognize the room. I've been in the infirmary.

"*For how long?*" I wonder.

My body feels much better than it did before. The pain in my ribs has subsided to a low numb feeling.

We walk to a corner of the infirmary I hadn't noticed before. There's a silver elevator. We stop in front of it, and the guard pushes in a code. 3-3-4-2-7-8-2. I try to etch the numbers into my brain.

When the silver elevator doors open, I'm shoved into the elevator from behind. With my back to the door, the doors close. To my surprise, I feel us going up.

I wonder if there's any way to escape. 3-3-4-2-7-8-2. I repeat the code in my head.

Then I remember how I got here. The fight with Emre. My plans to free the others. I can't believe I'm still alive. For a second, a stupid, giddy feeling takes over me.

Then the elevator stops. The doors open, and the guards lead me to another giant metal door. A different guard scans a silver badge against something that looks like a keypad, and a small metal piece appears in the door. Above the metal piece is a black screen with green light emanating from it. One of the guards takes off their helmet and puts their chin on the metal piece. The lights scan their eyeballs, and the door opens. The guards lead me inside.

"Where are we going?" I ask.

The security guard behind me jabs my ribs with a tool I can't see. I stumble in pain.

"You don't have permission to speak," the guard says.

The hallway is circular, like a tunnel. Black glass surrounds us. I can tell there are figures behind the glass doing things, but I can barely make them out. After we pass through a second set of doors, I see that we are in some sort of prison. On my left and right, people are tied to large steel chairs in cages. I can only see their backs because their chairs face a wall where images are projected in front of them. They don't seem to be able to hear or see me.

I suddenly become hyper-aware of my own breathing.

"*How do I get away?*" I think.

A guard gestures toward an open cell on my left. I swing my body and jab the guard on my right with my elbow, then try to run forward. But with my hands cuffed behind my back, I can't gain momentum, and I am tackled to the ground.

I kick and scream into the void as the guards drag me to the open chair. Metal pieces clamp over my arms, legs, and head, locking me in place. Then they leave me alone in the dark, silent room.

I anguish for hours, wondering what will happen, why I'm in this room, and what's happening to the others I saw. Eventually, I fall asleep.

When I wake up, it's still dark and silent. I'm still clamped into the chair. My body aches from the position I slept in, but I can't move my face or reposition my head.

"What's going on?" I scream repeatedly. "Why am I here?"

Eventually, my throat grows sore and dry. Hunger pangs set in my stomach. But no one comes. There's only silence.

I think of the old man and the little girl at my uncle's grave. I try to remember how he maintained the yard. I try to remember what he told me: *The world needs truth and healing.*

After what feels like several hours, I fall asleep again.

11

Who is Revel?

"Feonix. Feonix Cheenoma," I heard a voice say.

I wake up in a bit of a haze. The figure in front of me is out of focus. I squint and blink repeatedly to clear my vision. When things come into focus, I see it is the news director, Victoria Revel. There is a wooden chair next to mine. She is holding a metal tray with a white carton labeled *water* and a sandwich.

"I brought you some food," says Revel.

A mix of emotions washes over me. At one point, I had so much admiration for this figure in front of me. I remember drawing her image as a child and my uncle hanging it on my door. I remember crying when I learned of her illness. She represents so much hope and light. But now, I feel something dark from her. I can hardly recognize her.

She places the tray with the sandwich on the chair and puts the straw of the boxed water up to my lips. My pride tells me not to drink the water, but my instinctive thirst disagrees.

"Slow down," she says. "I can't really do much if you start choking."

She pulls the water away, places it on the tray, and then lifts the sandwich to my lips. I take a bite, struggling to chew and swallow. We repeat this process until the meager meal is finished, and a sense of shame takes over me.

"Feonix, I want to let you know we went through everything you and your companion had," says Revel. "Like many others who have come through this building, we know he is a spy for Rivers. But we are not quite sure what your deal is."

"You know, I've seen some of your work. As an editor, you've built quite the reputation here. You catch everything. You're smart, passionate, and resourceful," Revel pauses. "Like your father."

At those words, I look up at Revel's face. I had no idea she knew anything about me.

"Truth is, if I were really looking for a successor, you're exactly the type of person I would want. With no family obligations, your heart would be completely committed to the work," Revel says. "If these were different times."

At those words, my mind starts racing.

"But—What do you mean? The contest. My father?" I can only mutter words.

"Feonix, I've been ill for a long time. Luckily, we have some of the best doctors and engineers in the world at Station 7. They've kept me alive, kept the mission alive. But also, I've known who will take over this station for a long time," says Revel.

"Fifteen years ago, my team and I built something amazing. We brought light and hope to a dark world. We became the check on the powerful, and so we became more powerful than them," she sighs and sits down on the chair next to me.

"At first, I thought I might look to the masses for a successor. It seemed like a good idea, so I made the announcement. But then I realized that the type of people we were attracting just didn't understand that our mission is so much greater than simply putting out information. We have the influence and power to make this world a better place," she looks up at me.

"Your companion was right; we've withheld information at times. And for some, that may simply appear as if we are distorting the narrative. But we made a collective choice at the station some time ago that with all the knowledge we had, it was time to move off the sidelines, to stop hiding behind journalism, and actively make a change for the better," she says.

"But that means... it means you're lying," I say.

"NO!" Revel screams. She loses all her poise and finesse for about thirty seconds before quickly regaining it. I see something angry within her; it is seething.

"Excuse my anger, but I take such accusations very seriously. Everything we say is truth. We fight disinformation every day," she continues. "Feonix, we are building a coalition within the factions of people willing to fight back against rulers with authoritarian tendencies like Rivers, both here and abroad. That's why we don't publish everything. Some of those people are our allies. This is a new world. This is a war! We have to play to win!"

I try to shake my head, but I can't. My eyes look toward the ground with disgust.

"You gave so many people hope. Why the fake contest? Why continue the facade if you already know who will succeed you?" I ask.

"You know, Feonix, one thing that happened when I began this contest that I didn't expect was the types of people the contest drew out of hiding," says Revel. "The spies like your companion Emre—there are so many of them. Then there are the power-hungry snakes who normally would lay in the darkness with evil intentions, but this contest draws them out. Then, every once in a while, people like you end up here."

She looks at me with a sense of sadness.

"Your intentions aren't evil, but you don't share our vision at the station. The spies and snakes we usually try and execute, but for people like you, we try reeducation," Revel gives me a look like she wants to reassure me.

"Reeducation?" I repeat.

"We believe your heart is good, and with a little more understanding, you can learn and appreciate the goals of the station," says Revel.

Her facial expression turns very serious.

"We believe you can still be an influential part of Station 7," says Revel. "That's why I've decided to extend your contract as an editor for six more months. We'll see how the reeducation takes. Then, if things go well for both of us, we might offer you a permanent role in the station. It won't be my position, as we discussed. But you will be safe, comfortable, and able to continue the good work you've been doing."

A feeling of sadness comes over me. She really believes this is her best option. She really believes in what she is doing. Something inside me wants to fight this, to snap her out of it. I can't accept what I am hearing. I believe the station can still be the honest source of enlightenment everyone believes it to be. I feel intense frustration pushing away my sadness as I struggle to no avail to make eye contact with Revel while strapped to the chair.

"Just because you've convinced yourself of the righteousness in your public deceit doesn't mean you can convince the world, Revel," I reply. "The truth will come out, and people will turn against the station. It's been a source of hope for so many people for so many years. Tell them the truth yourself and turn away from all this. There's still a chance."

I almost can't believe what I just said. Revel stays silent for a few seconds, then looks away and begins to gather her things.

"We'll start with two months of reeducation," she says, turning to face me with the empty tray under her arm. "I really hope this works. But if it doesn't, you understand that our work, our mission, is bigger than any one person. And we'll do whatever needs to be done to minimize threats. As much as I admire you for being like your father, I hope you make a different choice."

"What do you know about my father?" I yell after her.

At that, Revel turns and leaves my cell. I hear the bars close and lock as her footsteps grow more distant.

She talks about him as if she knows him, I think to myself. *But how? How does she know him?*

Her words sink into my mind. *Our mission is bigger than any one person.* It is eerily similar to what Emre told me as he wrapped his hands around my neck in an effort to kill me. The memory of our fight flashes in my mind, and I let a tear fall down my face.

In less than twenty-four hours, everything I know and trust turns out to be a lie. I wonder how I plan to bring truth to the world when I can barely keep up with it myself.

For hours, my mind wallows in the new reality surrounding me. I wonder who the successor is. I think of the test we've all been a part of, the danger it put us in, and those who lost their lives.

"For what?" I rage. *"For nothing! They died because of Revel's deceit."*

At those thoughts, my fists ball, and I shake with anger.

While strapped to the chair, I waver between hours of sadness, hunger-induced defeat, and moments of determination. I try to remember the young girl at the graveyard, the old man taking care of my uncle's grave, the faces in the windows staring down at us. My resolve renews with each memory.

After several hours battling with myself, I lose track of time. I don't know if it is day or night when I fall asleep. I don't know how many hours pass when I sleep, but when I wake up, I learn what Revel means by reeducation.

The objective of the curriculum seems simple—break the students and remake them as Station 7 sees fit. But the methodology is intrinsic and wicked.

The first two weeks, I am basically forced to live in the chair. I watch hours and hours of videos detailing the history of the country, the crash, and what is happening now. At the end of each day, a man in light blue scrubs enters my cell and asks me questions about what I've viewed. He records my responses—or lack thereof—on a brown clipboard.

The first day, I am unresponsive.

"I'm afraid if you cannot open your mouth to speak, then you cannot open your mouth to eat or drink," he says calmly. Then he leaves.

The next day, hunger beckons me to respond.

"What did you see?" he asks. "What were some of the events occurring before the crash?"

"The world seemed to function smoothly," I reply. "But there were problems."

"What kind of problems?" he asks.

"I—I..." My mind fades in and out. I am exhausted, and all I can think about is food. The hours of video seem like a blur.

"I don't remember," I finally say.

"We'll try again tomorrow," says the man calmly. Then he gathers the clipboard and food tray and starts toward the door.

"WAIT!" I scream.

"I can remember!" I yell after him.

I hear the bars on the cell door close and lock.

"Wait!" I scream again. "I said I can remember!"

I scream repeatedly for him to wait, to come back, to give me another chance. His footsteps only grow more distant. After some time, I can only hear myself—my screams and tears. Then the parched feeling in my throat forces me into silence. Eventually, I sleep.

The next morning, the same rounds of videos play before me. I try to pay attention this time and remember if the images and lessons match what my uncle taught me about the world before the crash.

There are some differences. Revel—or whoever made the video—notes how governments knew how serious the threat of disinformation was but chose to downplay it. In worse situations, public officials used disinformation to attack political rivals.

My uncle never taught me any of these ideas. I suppose that is because many of the documents supporting the theories in the video appear to have come from stolen classified sources. Of course, these references aren't available to the public. Though I want to reject everything from the video, all the facts shown seem plausible.

The video also highlights the public's rejection of intellectualism, showing how, over time, the recommendations of experts are cast aside in favor of the opinions of online influencers and charismatic politicians with deep-pocketed agendas.

It depicts the oligarchical state that slowly erodes democracy in American society. The wealthy already wield significant influence over the powerful. But as time goes on, the wealthy *become* the powerful, changing systems, laws, and practices to ensure they maintain most of the wealth and power over the citizenry.

As the general public loses power and their conditions worsen, many rationalize with themselves. Some take to heart the statistics given to them by government officials showing the country is more prosperous than ever and wonder what they've done wrong to miss out on that prosperity. Others take comfort in their faith, believing that if someone is rich and they aren't, that person must be blessed by God. And who can question God? The list goes on.

But a few people rebel. Some protest the injustice and the erosion of their freedoms. But their protests aren't enough to beat back the consolidation of wealth and power by the rich.

It is against this backdrop and many other problems that the crash sweeps over the country.

My eyes grow heavy from keeping them open for so many hours. But the next time the man in the white scrubs comes, I am ready. I answer all his questions with ease. Then he feeds me and leaves.

This continues for two weeks. Then one day, they bring a mattress into the cell. I am given strict instructions on how I must sleep, wake up, and tidy the mattress each morning. I am also told that if I don't follow instructions precisely, the bed will be removed.

Under normal circumstances, I wouldn't have been so excited about a mattress, but as soon as I see it, I am ecstatic. Up to that point, I have basically lived strapped in that chair, only getting up to use the restroom. The idea of sleeping on that mattress feels like a dream.

I follow their instructions carefully, afraid of being forced to sleep in the chair again if something goes wrong.

Each week they add activities—sweeping the floors in the cell, exercising. Every activity comes with precise instructions on how to perform it. There are cameras in the cell, and I know I am monitored at all times. If I make a mistake or deviate from the instructions in any way, I don't eat. Sometimes my mattress is removed, and I am forced to sleep in the metal chair again. These routines help me understand what time of day it is.

Over time, the videos and post-video interviews become more intense. They begin to focus on the role of Station 7 in the current environment. The videos show how Revel is forced into tough, compromising decisions, but how she always keeps the public at the front of her decision-making. According to the videos, she always tries to do what is best for the people.

The videos also highlight the fraught environment Station 7 exists in. There are very few gray areas of understanding. Those against the station—like President Rivers or some faction leaders—are portrayed as outright villains. They sacrifice the people who trust them for their own gain and make every decision with selfish interests above the country.

In Revel's narrative, Station 7 is the knight in shining armor. It will restore order, accountability, justice, and financial stability while thwarting authoritarians and the rich—who have essentially become the authoritarians—to return democratic power to the people. If only people like me pledge our loyalty to the station and follow its lead.

I know what is happening. The station is taking me through its own mental and physical conditioning. They want to break me and remake me in their image. But I hold onto the memory of my uncle, the old man, and the young girl in the graveyard. I keep trying to remember them so I won't forget why I'm here. I don't want to forget what I really believe. I know if I can keep their images vibrant and clear in my mind, I can secretly resist this indoctrination.

But a month and a half into the reeducation, the routine changes.

One morning, after making the bed and cleaning the cell, I am strapped into the chair, and the videos begin. But this video is different. It is of me at work in the station.

My heart begins beating quickly. I know there are cameras in the building, but I never think much about it. Suddenly, I am very afraid. I don't know what to expect, what they've recorded me experiencing.

The clip changes. It is me in my bed, in my room. I suddenly feel nauseous.

"*Are they always recording me?*" I think. "*Even in a private, intimate place like my room?*"

I feel myself getting angry, losing control of my emotions for the first time in over a month.

I watch myself again, kicking and screaming in my bed. I can tell I am having a nightmare. I know it is about my family. Then I am eating lunch alone, arriving to work early, leaving work late, and editing. I look unhappy. I look alone.

But after joining the contest, my countenance changes. I laugh with Ray and Titan. I shake hands with Alex. My gaze toward Emre is full of love. It's as if I come alive, engaged in a way I haven't been before.

A tear falls down my cheek.

Then the video shows my fight with Gabby, me wiping tears off my face in the bathroom, me screaming in the night in my bed again because of the nightmares, me cuddling next to Emre in bed, then Emre and me fighting.

There are hours of tape, and I don't know what to make of it all. I feel sick to my stomach watching it. Then the man in the white coat enters the room with his clipboard and meal. He sits down in a wooden chair next to me.

"You have trouble controlling your emotions, don't you?" he asks.

"Y-yes," I stammer.

"In the past, you've put trust and faith in the wrong people, haven't you?" he asks.

"Yes," I say, feeling myself shaking inside.

I feel violated and embarrassed by the videos and his line of questioning. I look at the meal longingly. I have lost so much weight, but my pride will force me into starvation if necessary.

"You still haven't gotten over the trauma of your childhood, have you?" he continues.

"How do you live with yourself?" I reply. "Have you convinced yourself that this torture is justified?"

The man begins to get up and gather his things.

"Can't you see that everything you're doing is against the democratic values—like freedom—that the station claims so adamantly to support?" I yell at him. "Do you have a family? Do you have dignity? How can you do this to people?"

"You will sleep in the chair tonight," says the man as he leaves. "We'll try this again tomorrow."

I hear the bars of the gate close behind me. When I can no longer hear his footsteps, I begin to cry. I want to feel alone, even though I know I am probably being watched.

That night, I dream that Emre and I are in my old home. We are rolling on the hardwood floor, laughing and flirting. Then suddenly, Emre begins to choke me, and the twinkle in his eyes sets the home ablaze. I wake up screaming, sweating, and strapped to the deeply uncomfortable metal chair.

The next morning, I am given a bathroom break of two minutes. The timing is always short.

Suddenly, it occurs to me why they don't put mirrors in the bathroom. They don't want you to see yourself. They want you to see yourself the way they see you. I think about running, but I know I wouldn't get far and risk them deeming the entire reeducation project a failure.

As soon as I am strapped back into the chair, the videos from the day before repeat. I watch with the same feeling of nausea I had before. But I also decide to analyze my own actions more closely.

I got the job at Station 7 after my uncle died and lost myself in it. For a long time, I chose the comfort and safety of Station 7 over my purpose.

It isn't just the fact that I made friends that made me happier during the contest period—it's that I was doing something risky but meaningful. I left the comfort zone Revel is now promising to give back to me. And I was alive. If I am "rehabilitated" successfully, I will return to that comfort. But who will I be?

These thoughts scare me because I know if I feed into them, I might not survive much longer. But I also know there can be no other way. The way the stars align, only I can complete the mission I am formulating in my mind.

I wonder why I feel like I was chosen for this job. In the past, I often rejected the idea of fate. But while watching these videos, I know my goal is rooted in this calling, and the mission is bigger than any one person, including me. Contest or no contest,

I know I must take over Station 7 and bring forth the truth.

When the man in the white suit arrives, I am ready this time. I give him his answers, and he feeds me my daily meal.

"Your performance improved today," he says. "I understand that reflection can be a bit jarring at first. Tonight, I would like to give you a little bit of homework."

I am surprised. I've never received homework from him. He pulls a notepad and a pen from the black bag he carries.

"On this notepad, you will draft your confession," he says. "You've reflected on your actions, which show you as emotional, unhinged, desperate for companionship, and lacking in wisdom."

He places the notepad on my bed.

"These traits make you unfit for station leadership," he continues. "But because you've seen the error in your ways and are willing to redeem yourself, we'll give you a second chance to work at the station. This is the confession you must draft in your own words."

He releases me from the chair and leaves the cell. After I hear the cell lock and his footsteps grow distant, I get off the chair and walk toward the bed. I stare at the notepad and pen. My mind races with ideas. I wonder if there's something else I could do with the pen besides this homework assignment—like stab the man in the eyeballs or burrow a hole to freedom.

Then I remember the cameras. They are watching me. I sit on the corner of the bed and begin to write. In some ways, the words I write are undeniable truths. I am ignorant. And Station 7 is only doing what they think is best in a world full of evil and selfish actors. I can do better. I should do better. And part of me wants to return to the life I had before the contest, before Emre.

The next day, my confession is reviewed and approved. I am instructed by the man in the white suit to spend a few hours memorizing it. Then I am recorded saying it.

"My name is Feonix Cheenoma." With the video recorder in front of me, my lips mouth the words of my confession, but my mind is racing.

"*What was all this for?*" I wonder in my head.

When I am done, the man in the white suit enters the room.

"Congratulations. You've almost completed your reeducation," he says. "For this final week, you will be tested on your loyalty to the station. If you pass, you will return to your role as an editor. But if you fail... well, we'll explain from there."

"*One more week*," I think.

I am almost giddy inside. But I also wonder how they will test my loyalty.

12

Smoke, Mirrors, and Mass Surveillance

Back in the security center, Revel peers into the monitors at all the prisoners in their cells. Her fingers hover over the window with Feonix Cheenoma inside. She taps the screen twice with her finger to expand the view.

Feonix sits on the corner of her bed, her face toward the ground.

"Benjamin, are you sure Cheenoma is ready?" Revel asks the man in the white suit standing behind her.

"I've worked with her for weeks," Benjamin replies. "I'm the best instructor this place has."

"You didn't answer my question," Revel says, still staring at Feonix on the screen.

Benjamin pulls out papers from the black bag he holds and begins skimming through them.

"She's passed all previous components of the reeducation," he replies. "She displays a high comprehension of her previous lack of understanding and why that should change. Her ideology exam now shows her weighing the collective safety and greater good of the people over the pursuit of absolute truth. She has been through hours of loyalty training and has professed loyalty to the station. She is as ready as she will ever be."

"Sounds promising," Revel says. "If she passes the final exam, I still want her monitored. She's good on paper—too good. But her eyes betray her. I sense something there."

"What do you see?" Benjamin asks.

"I'm not sure," Revel replies. "It only flashes every once in a while. Looks like rejection, like resolve. Looks like she wants to kill you and me."

"You know people like that we can't reeducate," Benjamin says.

"I know," Revel replies. "But her followers have given me hell ever since she disappeared. 'Where's Feonix' was trending last week. This is the risk I take, pushing some of these contestants to build support online. Usually, I can predict when a contestant is getting too popular, but I was surprised by this response. It's strange—she comes from one of the poorest wards, has no family, and people can't seem to forget her. I might just be paranoid. I mean, what does she have left to fight for anyway? She knows that without the Station, the world is still nothing but chaos. She has no family. We are her best hope."

"Exactly," Benjamin replies.

"Let me know how she does on the final loyalty exam," Revel says.

"Yes, ma'am," Benjamin says and leaves the room.

When Benjamin enters Feonix's cell, she reviews the notes she has taken on the notepad he gave her.

"It's time," Benjamin tells her.

When she looks up at him from the notepad, something leaps inside Benjamin. It feels like a jolt from her eyes—the feeling Revel warned him about. But in the second he thinks he sees it, he's also sure it's gone. He wonders if maybe he's simply adopting the paranoia Revel had.

She stands up, and he shackles her hands and feet. Then he leads her out of her cell and into another room. In the middle of the room, there is a long desk with five desktop computers. He sits her in front of the second computer. The screen lights up in front of her as soon as she sits down.

"You will have three hours to complete the exam," Benjamin says.

He watches the perspiration build on her face, indicating she's nervous. He's happy to see that. She looks like a child, afraid and alone.

"Though you'll need the entire time, I would rush. This exam will decide your fate," he adds. With those words, he leaves the room, and the timer starts.

After several hours, Feonix's exam results are printed out for Benjamin. He stares at the paper in astonishment—it's one of the highest scores anyone has ever achieved. He thinks back to Revel's words: "too good."

He walks to Revel's office and knocks on the door. A woman wearing all purple with blonde hair answers.

"I'm here to deliver test results for Revel," Benjamin says.

The woman opens the door and ushers him in.

"Revel is expecting you," she says.

Revel's office is immaculate, filled with the kind of luxurious furnishings many people in the country haven't seen since before the crash. Her walls are covered in fan art of both Station 7 and herself. In one painting, an enlarged Revel speaks before a sea of people in front of Station 7, which is labeled, *The New White House*.

Benjamin rarely enters Revel's office, but each time he does, he's in awe of the place. The care in the decor and the talent in the art could rival the Smithsonian's collection before the crash.

"How did she do?" Revel asks.

"It's... It's probably the best score I've seen in years," Benjamin says.

Revel looks unnerved. She stands up from her desk and turns away from him to look at one of the paintings on the wall.

"I want her to remain in that cell another week and take the exam again," Revel says. "No studying for her this time. She stays in the chair, in complete darkness."

"Ugh, excuse me?" Benjamin replies.

"Are you using passive-aggressive language to question me?" Revel turns toward him now.

"No, ma'am. I understand," Benjamin replies, tilting his eyes toward the ground.

"Good," Revel says. "Leave those papers on my desk and get out of my office."

When I deliver the news to Feonix the next day, I'm surprised. I don't see a spark in her eyes or any form of resistance. She looks defeated, but she doesn't verbally protest. She simply walks over to the chair and sits in it.

It's strange to see. But I've seen worse before. Sometimes prisoners exhibit a sort of Stockholm relationship with the chair, enjoying their time in it.

I lock her in the chair. Then I shut off the lights and leave the room, returning only for short periods each day to feed her and allow her to use the bathroom.

At the end of the week, she retakes the test. There's no sweating this time. When her results come back, I feel shocked. My mind races. I wonder how Revel will react to this. Her scores are higher than they were on the first exam. I wonder if there's any way she could have cheated and conclude it's impossible.

I take the exams back to Revel's office. Revel lets out a big sigh.

"Release her," she says.

I return to Feonix's cell.

"Feonix Cheenoma, please follow me," I tell her.

13

Mapping Out a Rebellion

The man in the white suit leads me through hallways, locked doors, corridors, and down elevators into my new room. There are sets of white t-shirts and black sweatpants with the Station 7 logo on them on the bed.

"You understand everything that has occurred is top secret for security purposes," says the man. "Any disclosure of any part of this will result in a trial that will most certainly end in your execution. Tomorrow, you will resume your work at the station as if nothing has changed because, as far as we are concerned, nothing has changed."

I say nothing in response. I watch as the man in the white suit—my tormentor—leaves the room. Then I drop to my knees. I want to cry, punch the walls, and scream, but I know they are watching me. And I know I have to play a role until this is all over. I let out a big sigh, stand up, and head to the little bathroom inside my room.

In the bathroom mirror, I catch a glimpse of what used to be me. But now, I hardly recognize myself. My cheekbones are sunken in. My skin is dry and cracking. My hair is matted and tangled. I am completely disheveled. I am filthy.

I get undressed and take a shower. As the water runs through my hair and down my back, I let silent tears flow. I figure even if they are watching here, they won't be able to catch the tears through the water droplets on camera.

After taking a shower, I get dressed and head to the cafeteria for dinner. It will be my first real meal in over two months, and nothing is going to keep me away.

When I enter the cafeteria, I can hardly believe how normal things look. People are chatting, laughing, and eating, with seemingly no clue about the station's torture chambers above them.

"*Do they even care?*" I wonder.

They are fed, safe, and some of them seem happy.

I get my food and sit at a table alone in a corner, eating voraciously. I know people are staring, but I don't care. I am so hungry, and the food is so good I can hardly contain myself.

"Oh my God, Feonix!" I feel a hand on my shoulder. "You're back! I can't believe it's you!"

I look up to see Titan staring back at me.

"What happened to you?" he asks. I can see the horror in his eyes. "I hardly recognized you."

"Titan," is all I can say.

It's hard for me to trust another person again, but I can't help feeling comforted by his familiar face. Titan sits down next to me.

"Feonix, what happened?" he repeats, still staring at me in disbelief.

"I can't. I can't tell you," I respond, looking away.

"Why? Everyone's been wondering what happened to you," says Titan. "You lost a lot of weight. Are you ill?"

"Where's Ray?" I ask.

With this question, Titan's entire countenance changes, and I can tell something is wrong. Titan's head hangs toward the ground, and he stumbles over his words.

"He... he didn't make it out of the simulation, Feonix," he says, wiping silent tears from his eyes.

At those words, my heart sinks, and rage builds up inside me. I hand Titan a napkin and place my hand over his.

"*He lost his brother*," I think. "*And for what?*"

"Titan, did you finish the contest?" I ask.

"I couldn't," Titan responds. "I was too far behind, and I needed to say goodbye to my brother."

"Do you know what happened?" I ask.

"Currently, James has the highest score," says Titan. "Alex is in fifth. Gabby didn't make it past the third test. I heard it was brutal. Honestly, in my state of mind, I don't think I would have made it either."

I am filled with anger thinking about all these deaths. I look at Titan. He looks up at me.

"We were pretty sure you were gone too," he continues. "We didn't know what to think. No one gave us answers. There were rumors that you and Emre skipped the test and went away to live together or something."

At those words, a feeling of disgust creeps over me. There are so many things I want to tell Titan at that moment, but I know it isn't safe.

"So, you haven't seen Emre either?" I ask.

"No. We thought he was with you," Titan replies.

"When does the next contest begin?" I ask.

"Next week," he replies.

His voice lowers. "Feonix, what happened?"

I shake my head, indicating that I can't tell him.

I see the look of dejection in his eyes, the loneliness. It must have been amazing to have a brother by your side all these years in this dark world. It must have been amazing to know at least one person had your back. And they took that away from Titan. Now he's alone, scared, and completely dependent on the station.

"Where did you bury Ray?" I ask.

"He's in my room. I cremated him," Titan says, another tear falling down his cheek.

"Can I see him after dinner?" I ask.

Titan nods.

"When I lost my uncle, I felt completely alone for a long time, Titan," I say.

I am afraid to tell him this story. I never tell anyone this story. I am afraid that if he knows something intimate about me, it will make me vulnerable. But I recognize his pain. The death is still hurting him. And I know my words might give him comfort.

"He was the last close relative I had after my family was attacked and killed by the Patriots," I continue. "It really wasn't until I joined the contest and met you, Ray, Alex, and the others that I began to feel like a part of a unit again. And since then, though there have been some serious hiccups, I've thought of you all as my extended clan. So I want to let you know—you are not alone now."

Titan wipes the silent tears from his eyes.

After dinner, I walk with Titan to his room. I can tell he shared the space with Ray. There are two beds, two dressers, two desks, and two chairs. Ray's bed is made. I wonder how long he'll be able to stand staying in this room. There are printed-out photos of them together on a bookshelf.

I think about the conversations they must have had every night before bed. How they might have helped each other find things, pushed one another to get to work on time, and remembered each other's birthdays.

The room is filled with evidence of Ray's former presence. And I feel Titan's sadness. I wonder if it would be easier for him if he requested a new room, but then I also think he might not be ready to say goodbye.

He pulls a silver box with his brother's name on it from the bookshelf.

As I hold the box, I know I need to enact my plan quickly. I close my eyes, paying respects to Ray but also reviewing all I planned during the week of darkness Revel gave me. In the silence, I swear to Ray that I will not let his death be in vain.

After about five minutes, I put the box back on the shelf and give Titan a hug. As I hug him, his silent tears turn into loud sobs. Then I slip a note into his pocket.

As he weeps, I whisper into his ear.

"Keep crying and don't look at me," I whisper. "Only open the note in your pocket when you are in the southwest corner of your room. That is the blind spot of the camera—keep crying."

After another ten minutes, Titan's sobs subside. I hold his hands.

"I know this is hard, but it gets easier," I tell him.

As I walk back to my room, my heart races with fear. I know if they find out what I did, they will kill me. But I need to move immediately. I'm not willing to let another group of contestants risk their lives and die senselessly.

While watching the videos of myself, I memorized the angles of cameras in certain rooms.

Now, every time I enter a space, I try to identify the cameras.

I try to walk calmly, with the sort of sobriety one would carry after just leaving a funeral. When I enter my room, my heart stops.

The man in the white suit is sitting on my desk chair. He is clearly waiting for me. His black bag rests in his lap. He looks up at me and smiles.

"So, you have a friend," he says.

"Luckily, he's just a friend, or this could be a very awkward situation," I respond.

"I'm glad to see you are speaking again," he says. "You even seem to have regained... some humor."

"Why are you here?" I ask.

"Just checking up on you," he replies. "Some people have a difficult time adjusting back to normal life."

"*And letting me know you're watching me, going through my things,*" I think.

My heart beats intensely, but I try not to look alarmed or concerned by his presence.

"I'm sure it's even harder to adjust when you are showing up in their rooms unannounced," I reply.

"I understand that my presence may be jarring for you," he says. "But I need to do a small check-up on your adjustment. Please."

He stands and motions for me to sit. When I sit down, he goes through a series of questions about how I'm feeling, my attitudes toward the station, my attitude toward Revel, who I've talked to, and what we said.

Then, appearing satisfied with my responses, he gathers his things and walks toward the door. He opens the door and pauses.

"These check-ups will be routine, so you should expect to see me again," he says.

Then he leaves the room.

I take a deep breath, change into a loose t-shirt, and go to bed. I am so relieved I almost laugh as I lie down. Despite my anxiety about what lies ahead, I sleep peacefully that night. It feels like a gift from the universe.

The next morning, I decide to get to work early. My old spot, in the third space on the first row, is clear like it's waiting for me. I sit down and begin to work on a story about the environment—new predictions that government agencies are working to suppress, estimates that winter will extend into a sixth month this year.

I am following my usual fact-checking routine when James enters the room. Some people look up at him like he has already taken over the newsroom. Two female workers go up to talk to him before he reaches his seat. Then he makes eye contact with me and walks in my direction.

"I thought you ran away with your lover boy or disappeared like the others," he says.

"Be careful," I warn him.

"Actually, shouldn't you be careful?" he narrows his eyes at me. "I could be your boss soon."

"No," I reply.

"You know I currently have the highest score," he says.

"I know," I lower my voice. "I know a lot more than you do about all this."

I know I'm toeing the line with my words, but I need him to be curious and a little insecure.

"What happened to you?" he asks.

"If I didn't know any better, I'd think you sounded concerned for my welfare," I reply.

"A good competitor always tracks his opponents," he says.

"Well, you lost track of me," I reply.

"Technically, you're not really an opponent anymore," he says.

"Because we have all already lost," I whisper.

"What did you say?" he asks, irritation crossing his face.

I stare into James's face. Part of me wants to tell him everything—to bash his dreams. Another part of me wants to recruit him to help me. But I also doubt he'd even believe me.

"Did they tell you what happens next?" I ask.

"What do you mean?" James responds.

"Do you know how long you have to wait until you get the job? Someone could soon overtake your score," I say.

"They didn't say," James replies.

I can see the curiosity on his face. He's waiting for me to tell him what I know.

"James, I have to get back to work," I say.

"Fine," he says, turning to walk away.

"Maybe we can grab a drink after work," I suggest. "In the garden area. You can bring us some beers."

He pauses but doesn't turn around.

"I technically have plans, but I might be able to make that work," he says.

Then he continues toward the two women who invited him over with their eyes and smiles.

I look around. The workday is well underway. Emre's desk is empty. I wonder if anyone notices or will ask about him. I think of him, waiting in the torture chambers upstairs for execution. The thought makes me freeze for some time. Then I return to work.

At lunch, I find Titan sitting in the corner of a table. I walk over with my tray and sit next to him.

"Hey," he says without looking up.

"How are you?" I ask.

"I brought you something," he says, handing me a small bouquet of flowers.

"Titan—" I'm surprised.

"It's not what you think," he replies, staring straight into my eyes like he's trying to transmit a message into my brain.

I get the message and nod.

"Oh my goodness!" a voice exclaims.

Alex stands across from us with her own tray of food.

"I haven't seen you in forever, Feonix!" She sets the tray down, moves to the other side of the table, and wraps her arms around me.

I'm taken aback by the touch, and she can tell. It seems like it's been a long time since I've been hugged by anyone.

"Sorry," she says. "I was just excited to see you. I really thought something terrible happened."

"No need to apologize," I offer her a weak smile.

"What's going on here?" She glances at the flowers and then at Titan and me.

"It's not what you think," Titan says quickly.

"If you say so," she chuckles and sits down.

"Feonix, what happened to you and Emre?" Alex asks. "There were so many rumors."

"Honestly, I want to tell you, but I can't," I reply. "But I'm here now."

"Dude, seriously," she says with concern. "Are you okay? You lost so much weight."

"I'm fine," I emphasize. "How have you been?"

"Not great. In case you haven't heard, I finished fifth. So I'm thinking of signing up for the test again," Alex says.

"No!" Titan exclaims before regaining control of himself.

I look away, slightly annoyed that Titan isn't keeping his cool.

"What's going on?" Alex asks, looking suspiciously between us.

"You two spend too much time in the editors' quarters," Alex says with a smile creeping across her face. "Why don't you both take a tour of the control center where I work after we eat?"

The change in her tone and mannerisms is strange and abrupt, but I know what Alex is doing.

"Sure," I reply.

Then we both turn to look at Titan, and he catches on.

"Yeah, sure. I've never seen the control center before," he nods.

As we eat, Alex keeps the conversation light and humorous. She mentions she's seeing someone new in security and feels like things are getting serious between them—a rare occurrence for her. We laugh.

After lunch, Alex leads us through doors and narrow hallways. There aren't many people on the path except for two security guards and a janitor.

"Every time I go through this building, it's as if I'm discovering a new place," I think to myself.

We enter an elevator and go up. My knees quake at the thought of possibly heading back to the torture chambers. But the elevator quickly stops, and I regain my composure.

"This is the only elevator to the control center," Alex says, noticing my anxiety.

"It's fine," I say quickly.

After we exit the elevator, we walk through another empty hallway to a metal door. Alex punches a code into a keypad on the door in front of us. It opens into a wide dome-shaped room. Screens cover the walls, and people shout instructions at each other. They're so busy, no one even bothers to look up at us.

"This is the control center," Alex says. "We see everything here. Follow me."

Alex gestures for us to keep walking. She punches another code into a keypad, and a silver door opens into a narrow hallway. We walk about another ten feet before Alex turns to a locked door on her left. She pulls out a small key and opens it.

The room is tiny with screens showing security camera feeds. A big, brawny man facing the screens swivels in his chair to see who has entered.

"Hey, Jeff," Alex says.

She leans over and kisses him. I guess he's her new lover.

"I wasn't expecting you, babe," Jeff says. "I see you brought friends."

There's a slight sound of disappointment in his tone.

"This is usually... our private space," Alex says nonchalantly.

Titan lifts his shoulder off the wall he's leaning on, a look of disgust on his face.

"Oh, shut up," Alex says.

"Well, is there a reason we're here?" Titan asks.

"Yeah," Alex replies. "You all have something to say. This is one of the only spaces in the building without cameras. I know we're watched all the time—I mean, I'm dating security."

She gestures toward Jeff.

"I want to know what's going on," she says. "If I can fuck freely here, we can talk freely."

"With Jeff here?" I look at him intently.

"I trust him," Alex says, placing her hand on his shoulder.

"There's a very small chance you're about to say anything I don't already know," Jeff snaps.

"Then maybe you're the threat," I reply.

Titan touches my shoulder.

"Feonix, it's worth the chance," he says. "We might need Jeff's help."

"Fine, but I first want to let you all know that everything I am about to say could put all our lives in danger," I begin. "But I figure since you all are in the news business, that detail won't deter you. I almost don't know where to start, except that a few months ago, Emre tried to kill me."

At those words, I see the shock on Alex and Titan's faces.

"Geez, and I thought my relationships ended poorly," Alex remarks.

Their expressions become more serious as I explain who Emre is working for, the fight we had in my room, how I was locked away, the reeducation methodology, and Revel's big reveal that she already has a successor.

Titan slams his fist against the wall.

"Hey, easy," Jeff says.

Hot tears stream down Titan's face. He slams his fist into the wall again. He's about to do it a third time, but Alex holds him.

"It's okay, Titan," she says, wrapping her arms around him.

"But Ray—" his voice cracks as tears fall down his face.

"I know," Alex says, a tear falling from her eye as well.

"This all has to be happening on the 30th floor," Jeff says. "It's the only floor without cameras."

He pushes several buttons on the control pad, changing screens and security angles.

"I heard there were strange things going on there," Jeff continues. "But I had no idea."

"Feonix, are you sure about what you're saying?" Alex asks. "All these people... they're dying in a competition that isn't even real?"

"No, she's right," Titan says. "Everything makes sense now."

He rubs his hand over his forehead, as if struggling to think straight.

"Yesterday, Feonix gave me a note telling me if I wanted to find the truth about what happened to Ray, I needed to hack the station and search for files related to a reeducation program," Titan says. "I stayed up all night because I couldn't risk being caught on their servers, and I hid the drive with all I found in those flowers."

"What did you find?" Jeff asks.

"Proof for almost everything Feonix has been telling us," Titan replies. "There are documents, almost a curriculum, for the reeducation programs. It's basically a scary brainwashing experiment."

Titan explains that he also found a list of names of people who are being monitored after going through the experiment.

"And if Revel already has a successor, it has to be a producer named Kathryn Richards," Titan continues.

"Isn't that the name of the woman with curly red hair who officiates the tests?" Alex asks.

"That's her," Jeff says, looking up from his control board.

"Son of a bitch," Titan mutters, thrusting his fist against the wall again.

At the sound of her name, my stomach churns. My mind immediately flashes back to what the older man tending my uncle's grave said. A woman named Kathryn Richards was the informant who told the Patriots lies that got my father killed. So many thoughts run through my mind. Did she work for the government or for Station 7? Did Station 7 want my dad dead? Why? Have I been sitting under the roof of my family's murderer this whole time? Do they know who I am?

"Feonix, are you okay?" Alex asks.

"Uh, yeah, I'm fine. I just... I never knew her name," I say.

"Why do you think it's Richards?" Alex asks Titan.

"Her name is on everything, right next to Revel's. She has authorization approval for things after Revel. Every document is prepared so that when Revel is gone, she can take over," he replies.

"Okay, so what are you all planning to do with all this information?" Jeff asks.

I decide I want more information about Richards' connection to my father's death before revealing it to the others. I also don't want them to think this is just a personal revenge mission.

"What we do best," I reply. "I want to make it public."

Alex, Titan, and Jeff look at me with wide eyes.

"People are dying," I say. "And Revel clearly intends to continue this charade. This isn't a truth we can afford to keep to ourselves."

"That could destroy everything," Jeff replies. "Ever heard the phrase *don't bite the hand that feeds you*? This whole world is a sham. Station 7 isn't perfect, but it's all we have. We'll lose everything, and there's nothing out there for us."

Jeff shakes his head and looks away.

"I won't stop you all, but I don't think I can be a part of this," he says.

"Look, our work has always been about truth," I say. "And if there's one thing my uncle taught me, it's that throughout history, the people who defended the truth didn't always know what their actions would result in. Many, like us here, suspected the worst. And sometimes the worst can happen. But now that we know the truth, there aren't really any other options. At least there isn't for me."

"Feonix, whatever you want to do, you can count me in," Titan says.

"I'm on board too," Alex adds. "But now that I know what's going on, I'm afraid we may have congregated a bit too long. They'll be looking for you, Feonix."

"Alex, let me worry about that. Jeff, you don't directly need to be a part of this, but we could really use your help," I say, looking at him. "We need to know where the security cameras are located."

"Jeff, don't be a coward," Titan says. "My brother died because we believed there was a chance to run one of the most influential truth-telling entities in the world. He died, and so many others died because of this lie! We have to stop this."

"Look, kid, I'm no coward! I just know what's outside of these walls. Maybe you pampered editors forgot, but I haven't," Jeff snaps. "Shit gets real out there. You think a few people died in here? Imagine what's happening outside every fucking day."

"Jeff," Alex says gently.

"Alex, babe, your friends are making me sound like the irrational one here, but you know I'm right," he explains. "You can't just make everything public and hope for the best. We're in a constant state of perpetual war!"

"Well, then let's tweak the goal a little," Alex says. "We make this public and then take over the station by force."

"How are we going to do that?" Titan asks.

"How many names are on that reeducation list, Titan?" Alex asks.

"A little under 20 or 25 people," Titan replies.

"Well, then we'll start with them," Alex says. "We'll recruit them and any other prisoners we can get out of the 30th floor and lead an uprising."

"Are you fucking serious?" Jeff asks, worry sweeping across his face.

"We have less than a week before the next aptitude test begins. We have to start putting a plan like that into action today," I say.

"You said it yourself. This is war. We make this public, watch the place crash and burn as we take over and rebuild it the way it was meant to be," Alex replies. "We don't need to be living in the facade of truth and hope—we need the real thing, and that means we need to fight for it."

Jeff lets out a big sigh.

"This is not what I was expecting when I saw you today," he says to Alex. "But I'll do what I can."

Titan reaches down into the flowers and pulls out a USB drive.

"On this drive, I built a firewall, so we can chat and surf within a window without getting caught. It's still a little risky, so I recommend only opening the window when necessary," he says.

Titan pulls his laptop out of his bag and plugs in the flash drive.

"These are the names. It's about 27 people," he says, opening a document within a small window on his screen.

"I'll write them down," Alex says, reaching into her bag for a pen and paper.

"Great," I say. "Then we can divide and conquer."

"Feonix, I actually think it's best if you focus on recruiting people who are not on this list. They'll be watching you, and they'll get suspicious if you're in contact with several other people who have been through the reeducation program. It'll be too easy for them to notice a pattern," Alex says.

"We need to leave soon," she continues. "It'll raise questions if we're out of sight for too long."

"Okay, everyone, listen closely. This is the plan," I say.

In five days, Revel will take over all the airwaves to announce the beginning of the new aptitude test and introduce the competitors.

I explain that during that time, we'll need to find a way to hijack her signal, which Alex says she can do. Then, I'll tell my story, and others willing to talk will tell theirs. We'll release all the documents and stories online for the world to see and explain why we are taking over the station. Titan will build the website.

That same day, Jeff will plug a virus Titan creates into the security system so our location remains hidden for a while. Then he will put the building on lockdown before we move into Revel's quarters on the 30th floor, set the prisoners free, and quickly move to arrest Revel and Richards. There may be some fighting at that point.

"So we should be prepared for the worst," I say. "Arm yourselves."

"Over the next two days, we should work on recruiting as many people as possible, but you have to be sure you can trust them before revealing any information," I continue.

Before we leave the room, Jeff points out all the areas where cameras have blind spots—corners of the cafeteria, bathrooms, hallways, and other hidden places where we can meet and discuss what we plan to do next. He also warns us not to spend too much time out of the view of cameras. Security officials are trained to notice if anyone seems to be purposefully evading their sight.

We agree that Alex, Titan, and I will meet back in a blind spot of the cafeteria for updates.

Once we're sure we all understand what we need to do, Alex takes us on a quick tour of the rest of the control center. Then Titan and I return to the editing center to finish our workday.

When I sit down, I feel both excited and anxious for the first time in months. I realize I haven't sent a message to my followers in quite some time. It's time.

I write out the message: **Good to be back**, and attach a link to the climate story I edited earlier that day. Then I pause for a second and add another line beneath it: **In a world full of disinformation, only truth can help us hold the powerful accountable. Follow me for more of that truth.**

I take a deep breath and hit send. The message feels cryptic enough to go unnoticed by Revel and her team but engaging enough to gain some followers. More importantly, it means something to me. It also means I am still alive.

For the rest of the workday, I try to stay focused, but my mind races. I wonder if Jeff, Titan, and Alex know what to do or if they'll get cold feet. I wonder how many recruits we can actually get. Even though I think our plan is solid, part of me expects all chaos to break loose.

I look around me. It keeps hitting me how comfortable all these editors seem. If they knew the truth, would they really rebel with me?

Jeff's words keep ringing in my ears: *I just know what's outside of these walls.* I shove the words back down. I need to accept the fact that the only failure for me would be to do nothing.

14

Recruiting James

As soon as the workday ends, I gather my things and head to meet James in the Greenroom.

The beautiful underground space looks like an indoor park. There's a fountain in the middle and trees whose tops touch the high ceiling. I spot a couple making out on a bench next to a bush with little pink flowers sprouting from it. A guy in a hat sits on the grass, reading a book with his back arched against the stump of a tree. Truth is, outside these walls, you can't find grass this green.

"Hey." A hand slaps my shoulder, startling me out of my thoughts.

I whip around.

"Easy, it's just me," says James, throwing up his hands as if a cop just pulled him over. "I brought the beers."

He holds up a six-pack—clearly a brand from the cafeteria shop. They brew their own beer there and recycle the bottles.

"Great, then let's find a bench that's not already too occupied," I say, glancing at the couple who clearly need to take their makeout session to one of their rooms.

We stroll through the park, searching for a bench. I don't mind that I normally can't stand James because the park is warm and beautiful. I think to myself, if I die, this would be one of the moments I'd want to take with me. For a second, I almost forget the winter wasteland we really live in—and my real reason for meeting James.

"So, I've been thinking," James begins.

"Here." I point to a bench, cutting him off.

We sit down, and James opens two beers, scooting one in my direction. I look up at his face.

James is tall, lean, and even more handsome than I remember. His jet-black hair has grown and now just covers his eyes a little.

Looking at him today, I'm reminded of the moment we first met. I try not to stare too hard, even though I always find myself slightly mesmerized by his East Asian features. Those features tell me things about him that I don't even need his permission to know.

I know his ancestry makes it hard for him to interact without some discrimination from the factions outside these walls. I know it makes him more defensive. He either rejects those around him or tries to prove himself because there's always some doubt about the loyalties of people with his background.

"So," I say. "What were you thinking?"

"Never mind," says James.

He takes a swig of his beer.

"I see you're keeping your hair curly again," he says.

"Why do you care?" I respond.

"I like it better that way," he says.

"Well, I didn't do it for you," I say.

"Then that's another reason I prefer it that way," he says.

"I didn't bring you out here to talk about my hair," I say.

"I know, but we have a six-pack. I figure that warrants some amount of small talk," he says.

"I'm not really one for small talk," I snap back. "Particularly with people who have already let me know they have no interest in a meaningful engagement."

"Okay, I get it. I deserve this." James lets out a big sigh and looks directly into my eyes. "I was an ass, but at that time, I meant what I said. I wasn't your friend and wasn't going to try to be. I had a goal. Everyone in that room was competition to me. To think of them as anything other than that risked me getting vulnerable, letting my guard down, and possibly getting backstabbed."

I frown and take a deep breath. Inside, I know he's right and feel like a fool for not following a similar mantra.

"My entire life, I've felt as if the world was against me for reasons I couldn't understand," James says, taking another swig of beer with his eyes angry and cast toward the ground. "That's why I protect myself, and sometimes I do that by pushing people away. People I'm afraid could get through my defenses—like you."

I look up at him. His eyes are unguarded and sincere. He studies my face to see if I'm accepting his apology.

"I've experienced some of that myself, you know," I reply.

"Oh, I'm sure you have, but you have no idea how ugly it can get. It's one thing to be passively discriminated against. It's another thing to be hunted by people who hate you for being born," James says.

His words send chills down my spine. After the crash, everyone was wary of people they viewed as foreign. But we knew those of East Asian descent had it the worst. When I lived with my uncle, we heard rumors of bands of people who hunted, killed, and trafficked anyone with East Asian features.

"So, what was it like?" I ask.

"My family knew we were being hunted, so we did everything underground. My mother and father took every precaution," James says. "But it wasn't enough."

He wipes the dampness from his forehead; it's clear the memories overwhelm his body and emotions like my nightmares do to me.

"When I was 14, my aunt announced we would have a small family party for New Year's—underground, of course. We were all so excited," James continues. "Things with the hunters were quiet. We hadn't heard of raids, kidnappings, or killings in months. We were relaxed. We let our guard down."

James looks ecstatic, almost whimsical, as he describes how he and his family went to great lengths to plan this party. It's as if he can see his mother and aunt teaching him and his brother how to make decorations, his father gathering food they weren't allowed to touch until the night of the party. His family was poor, but they wanted to make that night special. My gut wrenches, knowing where this story is going.

"I'll never forget seeing my mother walk out of the kitchen toward the living room with the New Year's cake and a bright smile on her face," James pauses. His voice cracks.

"Then suddenly, the middle of her baby-blue dress starts to stain red, and the smile on her face falls with her body. A figure dressed in black with a black hood stands behind her with a gun in his hands," James continues. "I can see he's smiling."

James explains how, after that moment, all chaos breaks loose. Raiders enter through the window slits and doors. They slice and shoot at anyone who moves. His father pushes him and his brother toward his aunt and tells them to run. His aunt tries to escape, but when she realizes she won't get far, she pushes James and his brother into a closet, pulls jackets and coats over their bodies, and shuts the door.

"I held my brother's mouth shut and begged him with my eyes not to cry when we heard her dying screams outside the door. I don't remember how long we stayed in that closet," James says.

At this point, James has guzzled down his first bottle of beer, and so have I. His face is flushed, but he lifts two more beers out of the bag, opens them, and pushes one toward me.

"For years, my brother and I were all we had," he continues. "We were constantly shunned, denied work, and bullied on the streets. My brother ended up in prison after robbing a store so I would have better clothes for job interviews. One person was killed. He wasn't the one who shot the guy, but they pinned it on him."

James pauses and looks up at me.

"In here, we all have such strong moral compasses. We have these ideas about what's wrong and right. But out there, those ideas are almost foolish. If you steal bread because you can't get a job because everyone around you is a fuckin' bigot, are you really a criminal? Or just hungry?" James' eyes are stern as he speaks.

"Thanks to my brother, I finally got a job. This was the only place that gave me a chance. I was determined to make the most of this chance. I started out cleaning the floors, became an editor, and now look at me. I don't just do this for myself; I do it for my brother and everyone else who looks like me and can't get ahead. I've been betrayed and backstabbed too many times. After that New Year's night, I never let my guard down," he continues.

I can't look into his eyes anymore. When I glance down, I notice an ant crawling on the corner of the bench. I haven't seen an ant in such a long time. I wonder when they brought them in and how many other animals they have in this beautiful green space.

"I feel like outside these walls, there's so much hurt and brokenness," I finally reply.

"Look," James says. "I know everything I told you isn't an excuse for how I treated you. I'm sure you have your own sad story to tell. I see it in your eyes sometimes."

I look up at him.

"I just hope it helps you understand where I'm coming from a little better. I never tell people this. Shit, now I feel like I'm just rambling," he says.

I get up and grab another beer out of James' bag. Then I sit down beside him, just out of view of the room camera. James looks at my rearrangement quizzically.

"Look, James," I bring my voice down to a whisper. "You were right."

His eyes widen, and he gives me a confused look.

"I wish I had the discretion you had," I pause and take a deep breath. "About Emre. You were right about him. He tried to kill me."

James' brows furrow, and he shakes his head.

"Is that what happened to you?" James asks. "But you're here now."

"Don't talk too much. They can see you," I reply.

James narrows his eyes as a confused expression covers his face.

"Revel, they can see you from that angle," I whisper. "Emre is only part of what happened to me. Emre was working for President Rivers. When I found out, he tried to kill me. Your warning, despite its brashness, might have saved my life."

"I'm sorry," he says. "Not for the warning, but for how things turned out. I know you must have been wanting something different."

I almost blush at those words. I feel embarrassed and seen.

"No," I shake my head. "That's not the worst of it, James."

I pull his face close to my own until I can feel his breath on my lips when we speak.

"Uhh... Feonix, what's going on?" he says with a slight chuckle.

"I need this to look like we're talking about something different," I say. "James, I need your help to take over the station."

"What are you talking about, Feonix?" he says. "Goodness, you've only had two beers."

James starts to pull away, but I pull him back toward me.

"I'm afraid you and I and everyone else in the contest were backstabbed by the station," I say. "The contest, everything about it, is a lie. Revel already has a successor. She's pulled away from everything this station used to be. Truth is no longer paramount here. The station wants to reform the government and society."

"Feonix, get your hands off the back of my neck," James says, his tone cold and angry now.

"James, I have proof," I stare intensely into his eyes, trying to communicate how desperate the situation has become.

"I left a drive in your beer bag. Titan pulled it for me. Everything's there, encrypted. We only have a few days, and we could use your help," I say.

"Feonix, I think our time here is done," says James, standing up and pulling away from me. "I don't know what's gotten into you, but this is not what I expected."

"James, I wouldn't deceive you," I say, looking up at him.

I see a flash of fear and insecurity in his eyes. At that moment, I want to kick myself for being so aggressive with my approach. Then he turns around and walks out of the garden.

"*Shit,*" I think to myself.

My head spins. I can't tell if it's the alcohol or my stress. I pick up my backpack and decide to walk back to my room.

When I open the door, the man with the white suit is at my desk. I ignore him as I put my backpack down and begin changing into a more relaxed t-shirt and pair of shorts as if he isn't there.

"So, you've been strangely social," he says.

"Felt like it was time I turned a leaf, made some friends," I reply.

"Sit down," says the man. "Tell me about your activities today."

"I'm sure you already have the answers," I reply.

"I said sit down," he insists with a wicked smile creeping onto his face, hiding something more sinister beneath it.

I sit on the corner of the bed across from him. As he questions me about my day, I answer him, but with each response, my hatred for him rekindles. I imagine stabbing him and watching the deep red color of his blood stain that white suit.

"You went off our grid for some time today," he says.

"What do you mean?" I reply.

"For a second, we thought you disappeared," he says, staring directly into my eyes.

I can feel that he's leading me with his questions. The intensity of his stare is like we're in a competition, waiting for one of us to blink. I have no intention of losing.

"I didn't think that was possible. You watch me when I sleep, when I shit—what else do you want?" I reply.

With that, the man stands up and gathers his things.

"I'll see you again soon," he says as he exits the room.

I take a deep breath and fall backward onto my bed. It's like I just realized how tired I am. I'm so tired. I only realize I've drifted into a deep sleep when a knock at my door jolts me awake.

I glance at the time. It's 3:44 a.m. My heart starts pounding.

"*Who could be at my door at this hour?*" I wonder. I think maybe they've decided my answers weren't good enough and want to take me to be executed.

The knock comes again. I get out of bed and slowly walk toward the door.

"Who is it?" I call out in a loud whisper.

"It's me." There's a pause. "James."

I open the door and poke my head out.

"Follow me," he says. "It's not safe here."

He starts walking.

"Wait," I say, reaching for my bag and shoes, hurriedly putting them on.

He pauses as I gather my things. Then we're off, walking hastily between corridors, down flights of stairs, and through doors until we enter what looks like a janitor's closet.

I'm out of breath by the time we stop.

"How are you going to lead a revolution if you get worn out by a few stairs?" he says.

I look up at him. He's wearing a black t-shirt and blue jeans. His hair hangs over his eyes, messy but still handsome. His broad chest rises and falls, struggling for air.

"Shut up. You're just as winded as I am. You were practically running, and you woke me up in the middle of the night," I say.

"Relax, I was just kidding," he replies.

"Is this a safe space to talk?" I ask, looking around for cameras.

"As safe a space as any. No cameras," he says.

"How did you know about this place?" I ask.

"Remember," James shakes his head at me. "I told you when I first started working here, I swept the floors. I worked my way up to the job I have today. It took a long time, and now I'm considering throwing it all away for you. I mean... because of you."

I look up at him. I press my spine against the metal shelving and suck in a breath that tastes like dust. My pulse flutters in my throat. Being here, alone with James, feels more dangerous than it should. The overhead light flickers, casting faint shadows that shift across his face. For a moment, neither of us speaks.

The hallway outside is silent. It's late enough that most of the station's staff should be asleep, but I still expect footsteps any second. If security finds us huddled in this closet—especially with me—that's it.

James leans back against the opposite wall. He looks the same as ever: confident tilt of the chin, faint smirk on his lips. But there's tension in his posture; I can see it in the way his shoulders tighten. I've been watching people too closely these days not to notice.

"Go ahead," I say, keeping my voice as low as possible.

He exhales. "I'm in, Feonix. Whatever you're planning—I want to help."

I scoff, not bothering to hide the edge in my voice. "You want to help," I repeat. "Right. And you're just... what, risking your brand-new golden ticket? Don't expect me to believe you're suddenly an ally."

His expression darkens. "You think I only care about this score?"

"I don't know what you care about." I glare, crossing my arms over my chest to steady myself. "But I do know you're the reigning champion. You could walk into Revel's office tomorrow and get any job you want. Why throw it all away?"

He opens his mouth, probably to toss off some witty remark, but instead, he bites his lip. He studies me for a moment, like he's sifting through what he really wants to say.

"You don't get it," he starts, then glances at the door. "Look... Everyone else here sees how you push back. They might not say it, but they see it. And I—" He hesitates. "I've seen it for a lot longer than you know."

My heart gives a traitorous jolt. "What are you talking about?"

"That fiasco months ago in the editing suite. The rogue numbers? No one wanted to touch them—even though they were obviously doctored. But you refused to let the story go out full of lies. I could hear Brian cursing from the other floor. Remember?"

I do. I remember the trembling in my knees, struggling to get out of the room, but also the certainty I felt. They were lying to everyone—acting like there were no errors with the bots. "Why are you bringing that up?"

"Because it's the moment I realized you were... different. Braver than the rest of us." He shifts his stance, lowering his voice. "I used to think if I kept my head down, played by Revel's rules, I'd be safe—change the circumstances for myself, my brother, my people eventually. But after going through the files, seeing you defy them like that? I know this is the only way."

A tiny flicker of satisfaction rises in my chest, but I hide it. "You still didn't step in to help before, did you?"

He winces, gaze flicking to the floor. "No. I was a coward. And I kept playing the game. But now—" He meets my eyes again. "Everything that's happened with Emre, with the station covering up more stories... it's too far gone. I'm done pretending."

Silence stretches. Despite myself, I feel a glimmer of hope. I need someone like James—someone with influence and skill. But I won't let him see how badly I want his help. Not yet.

"You expect me to trust you, just like that?" I ask. My voice sounds harder than I mean it to.

"Trust me?" he echoes, a faint laugh escaping. "No. I'd be insane to expect that. But I'm asking for a chance."

He shifts forward, and I catch the light in his eyes—earnest, not the usual smirking confidence.

"Let me prove I'm not just out for myself. I—" His voice drops to nearly nothing. "I believe in what you're doing, Feonix. And I'd follow you if you'll have me."

My throat feels tight. God, I want to believe him. I need to believe someone isn't waiting to stab me in the back. I can't ignore the knots of mistrust tangled in my gut. Still... I can't do this shit alone.

"I don't have room for traitors," I whisper, stepping away from the shelves.

He lets out a breath, and I see relief flicker over his face. "I won't. I promise."

I explain to James what I know about the prisoners, the reeducation program, Revel's move from journalism to activism, and the successor.

"I have a team of people actively recruiting support for the rebellion set to take place the same day Revel announces the new games. We will take over the feeds that day, and things will get bloody," I continue.

"So you want me to help recruit people?" James asks.

"Yes. Here are a few names of people who made it through the reeducation camps. But I imagine with your current clout, you'd be able to attract more people. I would warn you to be careful who you talk to, but I think you already know that," I respond.

He nods.

"Well, I guess we should get going. If we're off the grid too long, they'll get suspicious," I say.

For a moment, we just watch each other in the wavering light. I can hear my pulse thumping in my ears. Then I nod, turning for the door. We both reach for the doorknob at the same time. His hand cups mine. His hand is rough, but the touch sends butterflies into my stomach. He doesn't retract his hand.

"You have to understand the gravity of what I'm telling you," James says, his voice low and serious. "I haven't trusted anyone the way I'm trusting you right now since my parents died that New Year's night."

"Well, you should know that I'm also taking a risk trusting you," I reply, looking up at his eyes, for the first time letting him see a glimpse of the hurt and pain I've tried to hide.

I hate that I can feel this primitive attraction toward him. I desperately want someone I can trust. The closeness of our bodies in this tiny closet only makes my mind wander. But Emre ruined me, and I hate that reality. I can tell he can read me, see the fear and want in my eyes.

His lips brush across my cheek. I pull away from him, knock his hand off mine, and open the door.

"I'm sorry," he starts.

"Don't worry about it," I say.

James leads me through all the narrow halls again until we get back to my room.

"Goodnight, James," I say as I close the door.

"Night," he replies through the door.

The next night, James and I sit side by side in the janitor's closet again, going through the list of names of people who made it through the reeducation camps. James managed to get a hold of a few other names, which he adds to the list.

"We need to split up and reach out to as many people as we can," I say, looking up from the list.

"We need to be organized, but we also need to act fast."

James nods in agreement. "We can't waste any time."

I lean back against the wall, thoughts of the rebellion, my family, and my need to know the truth swirling in my mind.

"Are you okay?" James asks, breaking the silence.

I turn to him and give a small smile. "Yeah, just tired. This is a lot of work."

"I know." James smiles back at me. He pauses.

"What?" I ask nervously.

"Your eyes... I hadn't noticed that they're actually light brown," he replies, brushing a curl out of my face.

My heart skips a beat at his touch. I've been trying to push whatever is growing between us aside, knowing it will only complicate things, but it's becoming more and more difficult.

"Let's call it a night," I say, standing to signal it's time to leave the room.

He gathers his papers, lets out a big sigh, and starts toward the door.

"It's really scary to start to care about someone else. For years, I've only really cared about my brother and myself," says James. "It's particularly scary because I tend to lose the people I care about."

His words send chills down my spine, like foreshadowing a terrible ending.

"Then maybe," I pause, staring at my feet on the ground. "Maybe we should try not to care too much."

"I've been trying, but I think it's too late," he responds as he exits the tiny room.

I don't respond.

PART THREE
THE TAKEOVER

15

Trust Is a Dangerous Game

The next few days are a blur. I feel a rush of adrenaline like I've never felt before. On the outside, Alex, Titan, James, and I seem to be doing our jobs as usual, but secretly we're aggressively recruiting for the rebellion.

There are 35 rebels and counting, according to my estimates. James convinces more than half of them on his own. I chalk it up to gender that people seem more willing to gravitate toward him as a leader. It makes me slightly insecure, but I also notice that he hasn't challenged my leadership like he did before. He offers ideas, but not before hearing my instructions.

Each night, I review the blueprints of the building Jeff manages to get for us. I try to memorize every hallway, hidden corner, and exit. But the building is so vast, so intricate. You'd never guess from the outside how deep it goes. It's like they're trying to create an underground city. I suppose that isn't a bad idea, given the possibility that war could ravage the country at any second. I know I won't remember everything, so I focus on Revel's quarters and other areas I deem essential.

I start planning who needs to be in each place on the day of the rebellion. As I travel to work and back, I make mental notes of where the security guards are. I also mark their quarters on the map. My goal is to trap as many as possible behind doors away from us on the day of the rebellion and fight the rest as needed.

I decide I need to be more active online. My goal is to build up my following and get people used to my voice the way they were used to Revel's. I want to appeal to people from my faction and build a strong base of supporters. And each day, I notice the digital world is starting to notice me.

Part of my plan involves sitting with different people at lunch so I don't attract too much attention to my core group. I listen to conversations more than I speak, trying to see if people are possible recruits. I listen to hear if they let disparaging remarks about the station or Revel slip. If they do it enough, I pry more directly.

But I'm always wary and extra careful because I know I'm being watched.

Apart from work and the rebellion, I find myself thinking about James more often. He also makes himself difficult to ignore. The other evening, he left a dagger with the image of a phoenix beautifully etched onto it outside my door. It's a nice thing to find after a long day of work and recruiting.

Then last night, he leaves the book *The Discourses* by Niccolò Machiavelli with pink flowers I know he stole from the green room outside my door.

This sort of courting is something I'm not really accustomed to. In fact, I don't think I've ever received flowers before. There's something a little cheesy about it. But I know it takes a lot for a guy like James to humble himself enough to try this. Then I remember there's a rule against clipping flowers from the greenhouse. The realization of his defiance makes me smile. I use a cup of water to keep the flowers alive on my desk.

That evening, a message pops up on my phone.

"What are you doing right now?" I see it's from James.

"Ughh,... working on the same thing I've been working on," I reply, realizing I have a big smile on my face as I type.

"Take a break. I'm coming to get you," he replies.

"James, I'm not dressed to go anywhere. And I really have a lot to finish," I reply.

As soon as I send the message, I hear a knock at my door. I shake my head and open it.

James is there smiling and stunning. He's wearing a fitted white shirt, blue jeans, a brown vest, and a brown fedora hat. His bangs hang from his hat, partially onto his face. He's holding a black leather jacket over his shoulder.

"Okay, this is not fair. Now I need to get ready," I say with a smile.

"What are you talking about? I woke up like this," he says with a chuckle.

"You sleep with a fedora on?" I ask sarcastically.

"Only when I sense something is going to happen," he reaches for my hand.

"Wait." I close the door on his face.

I rush to my closet and toss around the pile of clean clothes on the floor. I find my favorite jeans and a light blue tank top. It's all wrinkled, but fitted enough that the wrinkles stretch out against my skin. I grab a comb and run it through my hair, then quickly put on eyeliner and lipstick. Grabbing my jacket, I open the door again.

James turns away from his phone, looks at me, and smiles.

"You look beautiful," he says. "Let's get out of here."

He grabs my hand, and we walk through the hallways and out the door. The cold air hits my face, and I shiver. We rush toward a black Toyota, and James opens the door.

"Whose car is this?" I ask.

"A friend," he says.

I hop into the car. James goes to the driver's side and gets in. He speeds out of the parking lot onto the highway. I hold onto the side of the door a bit too hard, still fearful from my last accident.

"Am I going too fast?" he asks.

"No... where are we going?" I ask.

"Good, because we're a little late," he says, stepping on the gas and smiling.

James turns on the radio. I look at him and smile. I haven't listened to music in a very long time, and as irresponsible as this moment seems, I'm so thankful to be squeezing it in.

"Don't let go, you've got the music in you,
One dance left, this world is gonna pull through,
Don't give up, you've got a reason to live,
Can't forget, we only get what we give!"

We sing in unison.

James bangs his head back and forth. I burst out laughing. About forty minutes later, the car slows down, and we begin to curve along what looks like the side of a mountain. We climb higher and higher until we reach a place that seems like an outdoor club scene. We park on a less steep part of the hill where other cars have parked. James hands a guy walking around some cash, and the guy gives James a paper he places on the windshield. Then James gets out and opens my door.

"I can open my own door, you know," I say.

"I know. I just have never taken anyone out like this, and I want to do it," he says, smiling.

I smile back at him.

"Okay, I can accept that. It's kind of nice," I reply.

We follow the crowd on a dirt path to the top of the mountain, and I can hear the music getting louder the closer we get. The top of the mountain has been converted into an outdoor club scene. Torches line up in a circle around the mountaintop, keeping the place warm and lit. A dirt circle in the middle serves as a dance floor.

I step over a guy who's clearly intoxicated on the ground. There are also people in the corners shooting drugs up their arms.

"Dancing?" I ask James, slightly surprised. "You don't strike me as the dancing type."

"I'm full of surprises," he smiles at me. "This is my favorite spot."

He grabs my hand and pushes to the front of the crowd waiting to be admitted. The bouncer, a massive white guy with tattoos all over his body, including a cross on his right cheek, looks up at James.

"James! My man! What are you doing here? And who's this?" he says, turning his attention toward me.

"Feonix, meet Gene. He and I used to work the secret club scene together," James explains.

"Well, clearly you don't anymore. I thought you got arrested or something, but you look like a million bucks," Gene says. "You coming in? You know I gotta keep the line moving!"

"Of course!" James replies, walking past Gene and dragging me with him. "One drink on me later, huh?"

"You bet!" Gene replies.

"This area is where rebel youth and adults from all different factions come for anything—drugs, sex, dancing. I had a short career as a bouncer here. I had to stop after I got stabbed one too many times," James whispers in my ear.

I'm shocked. I didn't even know these types of places existed. People who reject the system but are still very much a part of it. A place where people can forget they're in a war. It's chaotic and cathartic at the same time.

James holds my hand and leads me around a corner to where the music is a little lower. We can see the woods, the sky, and the entire city from where we stand. The old White House and the memorials are visible in the distance. I know it's horrifying on the ground, but from this view, it looks magical.

"I'll get us drinks," James says, smiling.

Christmas-style lights hang from poles, and the glass surrounding the bar table and walkways glows in blue light. In the corner, a DJ plays music. She's beautiful, with rainbow hair that she swings back and forth to the rhythm of the beat.

James comes back with two beers.

"They brew it themselves," he says, handing me one.

"Is this a date?" I ask.

"Does it feel like it?" he asks, smiling.

"Yes," I reply, smiling back at him. "But I've never been on one, so I guess it feels like what I imagine a date would be like."

"Never?" James asks, surprised.

"No, never," I say. "It's beautiful up here."

"Yeah, it's my favorite spot," says James. "My brother and I used to come here after the clubs closed for the night and watch the sunrise. He used to say he could see Mom's smile in the sky. It's cheesy, but it's the kind of thing that kept us going. It hurts to think that he hasn't seen the sun rise in a very long time."

He motions to the bartender for another two beers.

"Slow your roll," I say, watching him crack the bottles open.

"I'm just getting started," he says with a mischievous smile.

I quickly finish my drink and take the second bottle.

"It's not cheesy," I say. "Seeing your mom's smile in the sunrise—it's beautiful."

"I loved my mom," I pause. "But when she was alive, I never really felt that close to her. It was as if she always had a shield up. I remember trying really hard to impress her, to get closer to her. But I always felt like something kept her distant from me, in a way she wasn't with my sister."

"Sometimes I think that's why I keep my shield up. I learned it from my mom. People think I'm cold and unfriendly, but I really just have fucked-up psychological issues from my childhood that I haven't worked through," I laugh—one of those non-joke jokes.

"You and everyone else in Station 7," James replies. "You have a sister?"

"Yeah, I had a sister. She was also killed in the fire when the Patri—" James covers my mouth.

"One rule here: no talk of factions. But talk of family is depressing, anyway. Let's change the subject. If you could go anywhere in the world, where would you go?" he asks.

"Why? You gonna take me?" I say with a smirk.

"Maybe. I'd go to the Greek islands. I hear the weather's warmer, and people are friendly. And with all this cold, I dream of beach days," says James.

"That sounds nice." I think for a moment. "I'd like to go to Istanbul. After my parents died, my uncle took me in, and he was a real history buff. He would tell me about all these empires that went through that region. I'm sure all the artifacts from the country have been plundered and sold, but I'd still love to see it. Plus, I hear it has beautiful mountains and beaches."

Something inside me lights up. I haven't daydreamed in years. I feel light and happy for the first time in a long time.

"Oh, history. So, the rumors are true—you are a nerd," he laughs.

"Not all of us can cross between brilliance and a club hopper," I reply.

"Brilliance?" he says quizzically with a smile. "Okay, I'll take that."

"What's up with the knives?" he asks.

"I need to survive somehow. Plus, it's a classier way to kill," I say.

"Classy indeed," he says. "Have you really killed anyone?"

"I haven't needed to. But if I had to, I would," I reply. "Usually a stab or two gets me out of whatever jam I'm in. Have you?"

"I've had to," he says soberly.

He motions for two more beers, pops them open, and hands one to me.

"What's your favorite food?" he asks.

"Ha!" I laugh. "I guess barbecue. You know I've been poor most of my life and had very few chances to try other foods."

"Have you ever had dumplings?" he asks.

"Uh... honestly, I haven't," I reply, a bit embarrassed.

"You're missing out! Next date, we're making them—my place," he says.

"Next date?" I ask. "You know we're about to embark on a mission that could get us both killed."

"But we're alive today," he whispers in my ear.

I smile at him. I take those words in—*we are alive today*. The song suddenly changes, and people rush to the center where the dirt dance floor is.

"I love this song. Dance with me," says James.

Before I can protest, he grabs my hand and takes me onto the dance floor. Our bodies flow together to the music. The snow starts falling, but the torches, alcohol, and the closeness of our bodies keep me warm. For the first time in a long time, I notice the different shapes and flakes within the snow. And even though there is snow, I can see the stars and the moon clearly at the top of the mountain.

"This is magical," I whisper in James's ear.

He brushes a snowflake off my cheek and pulls me close to his body. His chest is warm, and he smells amazing. We sway to the music. We dance until the DJ calls the last song. Then we find a corner on the side of the cliff and sit. Several other couples and groups are also sitting on the cliffside.

"How many people have you brought here?" I ask.

"Why is that relevant?" he says. "I don't ask you about your past lovers."

"I guess I wanted to feel special," I reply, scooting a pebble around with my foot.

"You are. You don't need me to tell you that," he says. "You need to know that for yourself. Feonix, you're the prize here."

"I don't feel special. I feel alone. Like if I die next week, I won't matter to a soul. At least your brother will miss you. Who will miss me?" I reply.

"You have to stop thinking like that. You are a born leader. Look at what you're doing. This mindset leaves you vulnerable to people like that bastard Emr—" he pauses.

But for me, it's too late. The sound of Emre's name sends a shiver down my spine. I suddenly remember how cold it is outside.

"*Was it my loneliness and fear of it that made me vulnerable to him?*" I think to myself. "*Am I opening up too quickly to James?*"

"I'm really tired. Can we please go home?" I look at James sternly.

"But it's only fifteen minutes till sunrise," he says, gesturing toward the sky. "Fuck! Look, I'm sorry. I should have never brought that up."

He reaches toward me, but I stand up.

"I'm ready to go now," I say, more forcefully this time.

James stands and walks toward me. He reaches out his hand and tries to touch mine. I push it away. A tear falls down my cheek, but I quickly wipe it so he can't see.

"Feonix, look, I'm really sorry. I don't bring anyone up here. Ever since my brother got arrested, it's just been you. That's because you're special to me. What I meant to say is that you're special to so many people. I see it online all the time. I saw it here. The stares. They're not allowed to take photos here, but I know people recognized you—not me. Even though I have the highest score at the station right now. Everything about you inspires people. It's like you were born for this, even though you don't seem to want it someti—"

"James! Stop!" I interrupt him.

The tears rush down my face now, and I can't stop them.

"Feonix," he reaches out to me.

I push him away.

"No! Take me home now!" I don't know why I'm so upset. Is it because he read me like a book, and now I feel completely exposed and vulnerable? Is it because I'm falling for him, and I'm afraid I'm making another mistake? All of the above.

We get into the car and drive away in silence. On the way, James tries to apologize repeatedly, but the last thirty minutes end in silence. The sun comes up on our way home, and I remember James saying he sees his mother's smile in it. I suddenly feel horrible for not giving him the extra fifteen minutes he would have needed to see that. I see a deep sadness on his face as it rises. When we arrive back at the station, James walks behind me as I quickly hurry to my door. I open it, go inside, and close the door behind me without looking back.

...

Four days after launching our recruitment mission, everything seems to be going smoothly. I still haven't spoken to James, and I figure it's for the best. I need to focus on the mission ahead of me. On my way back from work, I see another pink flower outside my door. I pick it up and throw it in the trash. I open my laptop and see a message from Titan that almost makes my heart stop.

"URGENT," it reads. **"Meet in Location 3 ASAP. We have a possible breach."**

We numbered locations without cameras so we could know where to go if we ever needed to meet in person. I delete the message, gather my things, and head straight for Location 3.

My heart beats steadily as I wonder what exactly Titan means by a "breach." It feels like hundreds of scenarios are racing through my mind.

Location 3 is in a gym. I want to slap myself for forgetting to wear workout clothes. Luckily, this gym is mostly empty. I go up to a treadmill in the corner of the room, a space we identified just out of view of any cameras.

The treadmills are old, but station engineers have done a good job of maintaining them. I turn on the machine and begin walking.

From the periphery, I see Titan approach me in full gym attire. Truth is, his stocky disposition doesn't help convince anyone that he regularly attends the gym and just happened to be here today. But I also think my clothes don't help either.

"Feonix," I hear Titan call out with a smile on his face, as if he just accidentally ran into me here.

I look up, smile, and wave him over.

He hops on the treadmill next to mine, turns it on, and begins walking.

"You look ready to work out," he says in a low voice, analyzing my attire.

"I know, I know. I panicked. What's going on?" I reply.

Titan's face turns into a frown, and he rubs his forehead as if he has a headache. My stomach begins to twist because I can tell from his expression that he has really bad news. I try to look calm and collected.

"Titan, tell me what's wrong," I insist.

Titan shakes his head.

"I thought," he begins, "I was so sure this girl would be on our side. That she'd be part of the rebellion. She said disparaging things about Revel few people were brave enough to say. So, this morning, I tried to recruit her. She said she wouldn't join unless she knew who was leading the operation, so I said your name."

"Titan!" I scold him.

When we began the recruitment operation, I instructed everyone not to give the names of other leaders. We figured if one of us got caught, the others would still be a mystery. Also, the less recruits knew, the less they could divulge if they were captured.

"I know! I know," he exclaims, pressing his face into his palms. "I'm sorry. When I told her, she smiled and said she'd need to be in charge, that she was already planning something. It was at that moment I knew she must be another spy for President Rivers. I called her out, and she basically admitted it. She also said they definitely had more people in the building than we could ever recruit," he continues.

Titan's words make my stomach curl. I want to throw up, but I know if my leadership is being challenged, the last thing I need to do is show fear.

"What did you say?" I ask.

"I told her that's not possible. She's either part of the plan, or she isn't," Titan replies.

Then he pauses.

"And?" I press him to finish.

Titan rubs his forehead again.

"Then she said we either follow her lead, or there will be no rebellion, and she'll make sure of it," Titan looks defeated.

My mind races with ideas on how to respond. I think about having her held somewhere until this is all over. Maybe we can use her as a hostage to make sure none of Rivers' agents foil our plans. Then I consider something darker—maybe it's better just to kill her. The horrible thought exits my mind almost as soon as it enters.

"Officiate an in-person meeting with this girl and me tonight. I want to talk to her face-to-face," I say.

"What are you going to do?" Titan asks.

"I'm not sure yet," I reply. "I need to suss her out, but I have a few ideas."

Titan turns off his machine. He actually looks like he broke a little sweat, though I don't think it's because of the exercise. He gets off the machine, grabs a towel, and walks away. I decide to wait a few more minutes before I go.

Back in my room, I have a hard time relaxing as I wait for Titan to contact me.

"*Would she really risk betraying the mission?*" I wonder. "*How far am I willing to go to make sure that doesn't happen?*"

I think back to Emre's words.

"It's my goal to put an end to the falsehoods and lies that drive our country into factions, making us weak and vulnerable. Station 7 grows more powerful while we as a nation grow more divided. The United States was once a single nation, the most powerful nation in the world. I've committed my life to restoring that," Emre told me that day we fought and were arrested.

"There's no way we can work together," I think. "Our goals are too different."

I hear the sound of a message pop up on my computer. I jump up, knowing it must be Titan.

"**Meet in Location 16 at 11:00 p.m.**," it reads.

I go over my options again in my head. I can't decide what to do, but I know I can't let her lead, and I can't let her screw this up. I'll do whatever needs to be done to make sure the plan isn't foiled.

I casually shuffle to the corner of the room where I know there are no cameras and strap a knife I stole from the cafeteria to my ankle. I use my jeans to cover the knife.

11:00 p.m. comes before I know it. I head to Location 16. By now, I've memorized my way through the maze of stairwells and hallways.

Location 16 is a storage space for food. The room is filled with tall metal shelves holding bags of pasta, rice, potatoes, and canned goods I can't immediately identify.

I wade between the shelves until I hear the faint sound of voices. I follow the sound. It seems like a larger group than I expected. In a clearing between the shelves, I see a small crowd of people gathered. Their voices go silent as they notice me. I see Titan in the crowd. He looks at me with relief and rushes to stand next to me. His expression tells me he's distressed.

"I fucking told her this was just supposed to be you and her meeting," he says, shaking his head. "If you want, we can call this all off. It seems too risky this way."

"Let's get this over with," I tell Titan.

"Blake," Titan calls out. "This is Feonix. She's in charge of the mission."

A pale woman with brown hair and brown eyes stands up and walks toward me. Her look is simple—she's not the type of person who stands out in a crowd, perfect for a spy. She's tall, at least 5'11". Judging by her features, I'd guess she's around thirty-five years old. The way she squints at me as she walks over tells me this won't be an easy conversation. She looks at me like I'm fresh meat.

"Feonix?" she says quizzically. "You look like a child. Are you the one supposedly leading this rebellion?"

"There's no question. This is my rebellion, Blake, and you're either in or you're out," I reply.

I don't expect to take such a brash tone, but something about her demeanor tells me there's no room to show kindness or negotiate. She chuckles.

"Feonix, these are just a few of the people I work with in this building," she says, tilting her hand toward the group of about ten people behind her. "We've been positioning ourselves to take over this building for quite some time. And we figure the contest is the best medium for that. We need the people to feel like the transition of power isn't a transition at all. There are just too many reasons we cannot allow you to lead this. So, I am taking this opportunity to allow you to step down."

I shake my head at her.

"*All these people, and they still think the contest is real?*" I think to myself.

"You know I can't do that," I reply. "Look, I know you think President Rivers will keep her promise to unify the United States and restore order the way it once was, but that is simply not true. A free media in a democracy must be just that—free. It cannot be controlled by the state and be free. Station 7, as powerful and corrupt as it is, is the only check we have right now. It has to remain independent for there to be any accountability. If Rivers gets her hands on it, she'll use it to consolidate power for herself, not the people."

"You have no idea what you're talking about, foolish child," she spits back at me.

"No!" I yell. My blood boils with anger. "You have no idea what you're talking about. You think you can win through the contest? Well, you have one big hole in your plan. There is no contest!"

I look around at the other spies for Rivers. They are silent, their eyes fixed on me, waiting for me to continue.

"Revel has known for years who she was going to pick as a successor," I explain. "She uses the competition to root out spies and people she considers too ambitious."

"Lies," she says angrily, but I see uncertainty in her eyes.

"Oh, really," I reply. "If you think I'm lying, go ahead and continue with your plan."

I turn to the crowd behind her.

"But many of you know what I'm saying is true. You also know that President Rivers is misguided and that I'm right about maintaining an independent check on all these tyrannical governments. They only use us to maintain their selfish grip on power," I continue.

"Look," Blake replies. "I wanted to be nice and give you an opportunity to work with us."

"That's not possible," I interject.

"Oh, I see that now," she says and charges at me.

I shift my body to the left as she comes toward me at full speed. Then I lift my leg and use my arms to ensure her stomach sinks into the center of my knee.

The crowd lets out a gasp, surprised at my quick reflexes. Blake holds her stomach in pain but doesn't fall to the ground. I quickly scan the area to make sure no one else is coming at me. Three of her people are holding Titan back, and he's struggling to break free.

I hesitate, torn between running to Titan to ensure he's okay or attacking Blake. In that brief hesitation, Blake throws a punch across my face. I grab her arms, and we begin to wrestle across the room, each of us trying to gain control. My mind flashes back to my fight with Emre, and rage takes over. I use my knee to pin her leg, giving me the second I need to use my body weight to hold her down. Then I whirl punches onto her face.

"I am the leader!" I scream. "You either follow me, or you stand down!"

Suddenly, a large object knocks me off her, and I slide across the ground. I look up to see that someone hit me with a bag of potatoes. Two guys charge toward me.

"*Not a fair fight*," I think to myself.

I pull out my knife and rush at them. I stab one in the leg, but the other hits my hand, and the knife skids across the room underneath the shelves.

A boot slams onto my hand, and I scream from the searing pain. Then I feel multiple boots kicking me all over. I try to roll away from the kicks, but I can't focus enough to move. Panic sweeps over me.

"*Idiot*," I think to myself. "*They might kill me.*"

I reach my hand out, desperate to escape the crowd. But as soon as I leave my face unguarded, a boot hits my bottom lip, and blood runs down my face. I scream in pain. I want to cry, but I know showing weakness will only encourage them. I wonder how much longer I can survive.

Then I hear a scream, and someone falls to the ground. The kicking suddenly stops. My attackers are distracted by another assailant.

I lie on the ground in a fetal position, afraid to move for a few seconds. Then I peek from under my arm. I see a tall figure with dark hair fighting each of Rivers' spies, knocking them out one by one.

At first, I fear the figure may be one of Revel's security forces again. But then I realize it's James. Relief sweeps over me.

"*How did he find me?*" I wonder.

James fights intensely with one of the guys in front of him. Then I notice someone coming up behind him. It's Blake, and she has my knife. Adrenaline surges through me, and I immediately forget all the pain in my body. I rush toward her and knock her to the ground, slamming her wrist against the cement floor repeatedly until I hear a crack. She screams and drops the knife.

Her wrist bends at an unnatural angle, completely broken. But I don't stop. I punch her until Titan drags me off her.

"She's done, Feonix," he says.

At the sound of his voice, I go limp. Titan holds me up.

"Fuck," he mutters, looking around the room.

Bodies lay all over the ground, bloodied and injured. The only person who seems unscathed is James. He punches another guy to the ground and stands tall.

"I could kill you all," he says, his voice calm, deep, and commanding. "But that wasn't the goal today, was it?"

The room falls silent. My heart races as I hear what's caught James's attention. Someone struggles with the lock on the door.

James grabs my hand and points away from the door. We run through the maze of shelves like mice. Behind us, I hear the clamor of Rivers' spies scrambling for an exit.

I know Revel's soldiers have entered the room when I hear shrieks and screams.

"Nobody moves, and nobody gets hurt," a voice booms through a speaker. "Put your hands up and prepare for arrest."

James leads Titan and me through the maze of shelves as if he's done this a hundred times. He lifts a hidden lock that reveals an underground space. Titan goes in first, followed by James. He holds out his hands, motioning to help me down. I start to descend until I see Blake wandering between the shelves, clutching her broken wrist, her eyes wide with fear.

"Get in here," James whisper-yells at me in frustration.

I think back to the torture rooms and everything Station 7 put me through. I know they'll kill her.

"Blake," I call out.

Her eyes dart toward me, desperate and afraid. I wave her over, beckoning her to hurry. She runs in our direction. James's eyes widen in disbelief as she slides into the hole. I follow closely behind, and James shuts the opening.

We all gather in the small space, silent. I hold my breath, afraid that if I breathe too loudly, we'll be discovered.

After about twenty minutes, the noise above us dies down, but we remain silent and still. I hear footsteps overhead. They walk slowly, clearly surveying the area.

"Looks like we're all clear," one voice calls out.

"Are you sure?" says another. "I thought I saw quite a few people run that way."

"I don't see anything, Fred," replies the first voice. "I've checked twice."

"Well, let's get going then," says Fred. "It's late."

We all remain silent as the footsteps grow fainter. The door slams shut, and the lights go off. Even then, no one moves. We stay frozen for at least an hour.

Finally, Blake whispers, "Thank you for saving me."

"Feonix," Titan whispers. "What the fuck?"

I can tell James is staring at me, waiting for an explanation. The room is dark, but we can still make out each other's shapes and silhouettes. I let out a sigh.

"I know what they would have done to you if they caught you," I reply softly. "I was on the 30th floor. I couldn't let that happen. I told you we have the same enemy, for now at least."

"I was a fool for bringing so many of them here," Blake mutters. "So, it's true? The contest isn't real?" she asks, looking at James.

"No, it isn't," Titan says sharply.

"How is it possible that we haven't heard this, but you all know?" Blake asks.

"I was on the 30th floor, tortured. Revel told me herself. When I got out, Titan hacked their systems and confirmed everything," I explain.

"Look, I'm sorry," Blake admits. "I'm such an idiot. I should've never brought all those people. We honestly thought we could recruit you all."

I chuckle, but it reminds me that my entire body is throbbing with pain.

"Like you thought you could intimidate me into joining you?" I ask.

"Yes," Blake admits, casting her eyes down.

"Then you're a fool, Blake," Titan says. "And now your friends are probably going to die."

I hear what sounds like tears coming from her direction.

"Look, you're right," she says. "I really fucked this one up. But if I promise to help and get anyone willing to join me to help the mission, can you pardon them at the end of this?"

"How can we trust you?" James asks.

"My younger sister might have been caught in that group tonight," Blake pauses, trying to hold back tears. "I'll do anything."

James and Titan remain silent. I know this is a soft spot for them.

"Then you're in," I say. "But the pardon will be done in the form of an exchange."

"Exchange?" Blake asks.

"Yes," I reply. "President Rivers has James's brother in prison. We'll release her spies in exchange for James's brother."

James seems to hold his breath for a moment, surprised by my words.

"I can't guarantee she'll agree, but I'll do whatever I can to try," Blake says.

Blake pulls out a round device from her pocket. It looks like an old compass on the outside, but when she presses her finger on it, it lights up.

"This is a communication device," she says. "I'm going to ask my people on the outside to make sure we're safe before we leave. They should also be able to tamper with the camera footage, so it looks like we never left our rooms."

"James, how did you know where to find me?" I ask.

"Oh, I might've mentioned our plan to him," Titan says sheepishly.

I shoot Titan an angry look.

"Hey, Feonix, don't get mad at him," James says. "I wasn't actually planning to get involved, but when you took so long, I decided to check on things. Besides, as brilliant as you are, fighting isn't exactly your strength."

I glare at him, wanting to be cold and distant, but then I remember he just saved my life. A smile creeps across his face like he can read my mind. I make an attempt to push him, but he catches my hand before I can. Then he slowly releases it.

I haven't felt his touch in days, and it feels like forever. Despite my best efforts to remain distant, butterflies stir in my stomach. I narrow my eyes at him, but I smile back. He reaches over and gently wipes the blood from my bottom lip.

My mind flashes back to our nights in the closet and dancing on the mountaintop. For a moment, I wish we were alone. I can see in his eyes that he's thinking the same thing.

"Well, I appreciate the help," I say, turning my face away.

Titan looks at both of us suspiciously. I can tell he wants to comment but decides not to.

"How did you know this hole was here, James?" Titan asks.

"Been here a while. You know I started at this station as a janitor. I've cleaned this room before," James replies, looking around.

"Blake, why President Rivers? Why did you decide to work for her?" I ask, changing the subject.

"I was recruited," she says. "She came to our village and offered my sister and me a better life. My parents had nothing, and we had nothing to lose. They took us in, fed us three meals a day—something we hadn't had before—and gave us assignments."

Blake shrugs. Then her compass-like device buzzes. She pulls it out of her pocket.

"Okay, they're saying we'll have a three-minute window to get out of here and back to our rooms in approximately ten minutes," Blake says. "Let's stay in contact." She hands Titan and me a compass-like device.

She looks at James.

"Sorry, I only brought two tonight, but I'll bring one for you later," she says. "It allows us all to communicate securely."

"I figured," James replies.

A couple of minutes pass, and we wait in silence for Blake's signal. My heart races. I retrace my steps in my mind, calculating how long it will take to return to my room.

"Now!" Blake whispers.

James opens the covering to the room, and Titan climbs out first. Then Titan and James help Blake and me out of the hole. We hurry out of the room, one after the other. Then we all split up, taking separate hallways toward our respective rooms.

Time ticks in my head.

"*One minute gone*," I think.

I try to run, but my body throbs with pain.

"Don't stop, keep going, Feonix," I tell myself, desperate and fearful.

But with the next step, a searing pain tears across my whole body, and I collapse to my knees. My heart sinks because I know this fall could be my death. I try to get up, but the pain holds me down.

As soon as I hit the ground, I feel a hand lift me up and carry my body as if I weigh nothing. I don't have to look up to know it's James. I recognize the sound of his heavy breathing as he runs through the hallways. I wrap my hands tightly around his neck and bury my face into his chest. I lose track of time in my mind, but we finally make it to a room.

He closes the door behind us and slumps to the ground with me in his arms.

"Why are you so stubborn," he says, lifting my face with his hand and wiping my hair away from my eyes.

"Wow, twice in one night," I reply. "You literally saved me twice in one night."

"And I'd do it fifty more times," he says. "But I wish you would just tell me when you need help instead of making me guess. It doesn't make you weak, if that's what you're thinking. You took quite the beating a few hours ago. You need time to heal. For all you know, you may have broken something."

"Okay, Dad," I reply sarcastically, indicating that I need him to tone down the lecture.

His words take me back a little. I find it hard to believe that anyone would risk themselves that many times for me, but somehow I feel that his promise to be there and rescue me is sincere. I feel my heart open up to him a little. And that realization scares me.

I push myself out of his arms and sit on the ground, against the wall, about three feet away from him. Then I finally notice that we're actually in his room, not mine.

I look around the room. It's neat and organized, a stark contrast to my own. There are ink drawings all over the walls with people's faces. The faces resemble James', and I figure they must be family members.

"Did you draw these?" I ask.

"Yeah, helps me to remember them. I couldn't save any photos," he replies.

"Is that your mother?" I point to one of the drawings above his desk.

"Yes, or at least it's what I remember of her face," he replies, looking at the photo.

"She's beautiful. You're an amazing artist," I smile at him.

"I wouldn't say amazing. This is more like..." he pauses, "like therapy. If you know what I mean."

I nod.

I stand up and look at the photos. Then I notice a sketch on his desk. It's a beautiful city with a seaport, a large mosque, ferries, and seagulls. Homes cover the hilly mountainsides.

"Is this—" I start.

"Oh, you weren't supposed to see that yet. It's not finished," says James. "Look, I know I can't take you to Istanbul any time soon. But I thought I could bring it to you. And here in this image, it's still beautiful. All the artifacts and relics are still there."

I stare at the photo and feel my hand shaking. I steady myself by using my finger to trace the details. I suddenly feel a pang of sadness knowing we may die this week and this dream—his dream—and everything we have will be gone.

"This is beautiful," I whisper as a tear falls down my face.

"I'm sorry. I would never purposely hurt you," he says.

"No, I'm sorry. You took me to the mountain to share something with me that you don't share with anyone. You were willing to show the vulnerability that I was afraid to," I say. "And I'm sorry that we may not live long enough to see that sunrise again."

This time James stiffens up. I know that realization has been in his mind, but me saying it out loud must have brought the pain out.

"I could really use a drink right now," he says, looking around.

"James, you can't drink away the pain. It will never leave you," I say, this time wiping two tears from his eyes.

He turns away. We stand together, teary-eyed and in silence for a while.

"You can have the bed," he says as he lays out a blanket for himself on the floor. "Like you said, we have a lot to do tomorrow. We better get some rest."

I look down. My hands and legs are still bruised and bleeding.

"Can I take a shower? I feel like shit."

"Of course." James gets up and pulls a clean towel, a t-shirt, and shorts from his closet. "Follow me. But leave your shoes by the door."

I smile at his request but take off my shoes and follow him. I still feel some pain in my side when I bend over, and I silently pray that nothing is broken.

The bathroom is in the left corner of the room. Again, everything is neat and organized. The white tile is spotless. I see myself in the mirror as I pass it and cringe at my appearance. My hair is wild and unkempt, and my clothes are filthy. I smooth down my hair a little, embarrassed that James has seen me this way. He doesn't seem to notice.

"I'm kind of creeped out by how neat you are," I say.

James laughs.

"It gives me peace of mind," he says. "I feel that people who have stories like ours either try to do everything to keep themselves sane or completely fall apart. Cleaning and art are how I keep myself sane."

He leans over the bathtub.

"So if you want to make the water hot, turn it to the left. If you want it colder, turn it to the right," he says.

Then he turns on the shower and touches the water to make sure it isn't too hot. He adjusts the knob again and puts his hand under the running water one more time before looking satisfied.

I chuckle. "I know how to set my own shower temperature, you know."

"I was jus—" Then, as if he realizes how silly it seems, he stops talking, and his cheeks blush. "I was just making sure."

He places the towel and the shirt on the sink counter and starts to head out of the bathroom. Without thinking, I grab his arm.

He turns to look at me but doesn't say a word. For almost thirty seconds, we just stare into each other's eyes in silence. Then I use both my hands to pull his face toward mine, and when our lips meet, my entire body feels warm like the night we danced out in the snow.

It's as if the pulsing feeling of want we've kept for one another is finally unleashed, and we immediately lose complete control. Somewhere between our desperate kisses, my shirt and pants end up on the floor. Then his.

We stumble backward into the shower. I throw my head back as the warm water runs through my hair and down my body.

"*It's the perfect temperature,*" I think to myself and smile.

James' face buries into my neck with kisses. I feel his rough hands unhook my bra. It falls onto the wet floor.

We pause for a second, both naked with the shower water pouring over us like rain. We are both breathing heavily. The weight of the water makes James' hair appear straight, while my curls get a wet spring in them.

"You're beautiful," he says.

"You are too," I reply.

"Feonix," he pauses.

I look into his eyes expectantly.

"I think I've fallen completely in love with you," he says.

I pull his face close to mine, and we begin kissing again, each kiss deeper and more passionate than the one before. I feel adrenaline take over him as he softly bites my bottom lip, then pushes my body against the wall. I feel a slight bit of pain, but the want in my body for him overtakes it.

He uses both hands to lift my thighs, taking me off the ground. My back steadies against the wall, and I wrap my arms around his neck.

The feeling sends sparks around my body. I throw my head up and to the side as my breathing intensifies. His grip on my thighs tightens. I don't know how much time passes before every inch of my body tenses, my muscles contract, and I pulse against him. Then, feeling my pulses, his whole body tenses. He lets out a loud moan.

My arms loosen from around his neck as he slowly lowers my body to the ground. We finish our shower together with silent smiles.

16

The War for Public Opinion

A giant thud at the door startles me awake. Before I can understand what's going on, I see several of Revel's security forces storm into the room. James immediately jumps out of bed and into a fighting stance, using one hand to pull me up behind him.

I look around. At least 20 security officers in white suits with guns surround us. I'm wearing an oversized T-shirt and shorts borrowed from James, and he's shirtless with loose sweatpants on. We're in no position to fight. My heart feels like it will beat out of my chest. My mind turns hazy for a second.

I wonder, *What time is it? Why are they here?*

Then, I think back to yesterday. I remember Blake and the raid. One of the people they captured must have talked. Maybe Revel knows everything now. She's definitely going to try to kill me. My heart sinks as I prepare myself with the few seconds I have to turn myself in.

I raise my hands in surrender, but to my confusion, the officers charge at James. They knock him to the ground, and he yells out in pain. I scream and rush toward him, but multiple guards hold me back.

"Let him go!" I scream. "You're hurting him!"

I kick with all my strength at one of the guards holding me, knocking him to the ground. But two others immediately knock me down and pin me as the others carry James away.

I thrash and scream, though my body throbs with pain.

"Where are you taking him?" I yell.

"That's no longer your concern," says one of the officers through his mask.

To my shock, they release their grip on me and leave the room. My mind races as I look around.

Why did they take James and not me?

I gather my things and some of James's, then bolt out the door toward my room. I slow down when I see security forces everywhere. I try to catch my breath and look casual. As I turn the corner to my hallway, a security officer steps in front of me.

"Excuse me, ma'am, where are you headed?" the officer asks.

"Uh, back to my room," I reply.

The officer looks me over. "Which room are you in?"

"318," I answer.

The officer eyes my outfit. "Go ahead," she says, nudging me forward.

I take a deep breath and briskly walk to my room. Once inside, I hide in the one corner I know isn't visible to the cameras. I open the compass messenger Blake gave to Titan and me and press my thumb onto the device. It activates, projecting a blue light into the space in front of me. Messages pop up like crazy.

"**EMERGENCY! WE HAVE A LEAKER!**" reads one message.

"**DAKOTO SMITH HAS BEEN COMPROMISED. JAMES HAN HAS BEEN COMPROMISED. LEONARDO BEARD HAS BEEN COMPROMISED. LARA GREY HAS BEEN COMPROMISED.**" The messages flash red in front of me.

"**IMMEDIATELY HEAD FOR AN EMERGENCY EXIT! WE REPEAT, IMMEDIATELY HEAD FOR AN EMERGENCY EXIT!**" the messages continue.

"**REVEL IS PLANNING TO ISSUE A BUILDING-WIDE LOCKDOWN. THEY WILL BE SEARCHING FOR SUSPICIOUS BEHAVIOR OF ANY KIND. HEIGHTENED SECURITY FOR THE NEXT WEEK. ALL MOVEMENTS AND GATHERINGS WILL REQUIRE PRIOR APPROVAL.**"

My mind races. I want to slap myself for not checking this earlier. I open my laptop and the secure window Titan created.

"**What the fuck is going on?!!!**" I see a message from Alex.

"**It's a long story,**" I type back. "**We had a mix-up with spies from President Rivers last night. Then Revel's security forces raided. Some people were caught. Looks like one of them leaked some information, though it was probably inaccurate. They arrested James earlier, but they let me go.**"

"**WHATT????? How could you all not tell me this?**" she replies.

Another message flashes from Titan: "**Feonix! What's going on? I'm trying to reach James, but there's no response! Do you know if he got out? I got the messages from the Rivers team!**"

"**He was arrested earlier,**" I reply, my heart sinking.

"**FUCK!!**" Titan writes.

I open a new window to include both Alex and Titan in one message.

"**We have to move quickly. I know where they've taken James,**" I write.

"**What do you want to do?**" Alex asks. "**I hear they're looking for traitors and any suspicious activity or gathering.**"

I weigh my options. If we move now, it could get bloody fast. We could lose so many people. Their defenses are up, and we don't have the element of surprise. Their blood would be on my hands. We could wait for a bigger audience, and it might be safer with less security once their guard is down.

Another blue-light message pops up from the compass device: "**REVEL PLANS TO EXECUTE ALL CAPTURED TRAITORS TONIGHT.**"

My heart sinks. I think of James, Blake's sister, and even Emre.

"**We have to move tonight**," I tell Titan and Alex. "**They're planning to move forward with executions.**"

"**Shit**," Titan writes. "**Shit, shit, shit!**"

"**And even if that weren't the case**," I continue, "**someone else is going to talk. Revel won't stop until she knows everything. They might come for us before we're ready, and that would destroy any chance we have at fulfilling this mission and rescuing James. We don't have a choice. We have to enact the plan today. We've pledged support from Rivers' people.**"

"**The same ones who are spilling their guts to Revel right now?!!**" Alex responds.

"**I don't completely trust them either, but right now, we need an ally. I'm going to take what I can get**," I reply.

"**But how are we going to move around undetected**?" asks Titan.

"**I have an idea. Give me 15 minutes**," I answer.

I look at the time. It is 3 p.m. I wonder how I could have slept so late with James.

"*Idiot*," I think to myself.

I open the compass-like gadget.

"**Blake, if there is any hope of saving anyone, we need to enact a modified version of our plan to take over the station tonight**," I send in a message to Blake.

"**I know... you're right**," she replies. "**What's the plan?**"

"**We'll put the plan in place at 5:50 p.m., right before the nightly newscast at 6 p.m. Can you get security force uniforms for everyone on my team and yours?**" I ask. "**We need them ASAP.**"

"**I don't know if we have that many, but I'll see what I can do**," Blake responds.

"**Also, if you have anything that can help with injuries... I could use it**," I add.

"**Oh, we got you on that one**," Blake replies.

I send her a list of names so she knows who to send uniforms to.

"**Please alert all of your recruits that we are putting the plan in motion at 5:50 p.m., right before the nightly newscast at 6 p.m.**

They should remain alert, as I will send instructions frequently until then,"** I write to Titan and Alex.

"**Almost everyone should be receiving security force uniforms,**" I continue. "**This should allow us all to get in place without too much suspicion.**"

"**Got it**," they both reply in succession.

I take another deep breath and lean against the wall. Then, I decide I need to get up and prepare for this fight. I change into jeans and a shirt. Then I strap two knives on either side of my body.

I hear a knock at the door. My heart starts pulsing, and I grip the knife at my side.

"*If they come for me,*" I think, "*I'll go down fighting.*"

"Who is it?" I call out.

"Security, open up!" a voice replies.

I take a deep breath and unlock the door. A security soldier quickly enters the room and closes the door.

"This package is for you," the soldier says.

I slowly take the package from the soldier. Then I look at the soldier a little more closely and smile—one of Rivers' spies.

"Thank you," I reply.

The soldier nods and leaves.

I take the box to a corner of the room where I know the camera cannot see me and open it. Inside, there's a white security force uniform, a bottle of liquid, a gun, and a black cloth.

A note attached to the liquid bottle reads: *Use this to dampen the cloth and rub over wounded areas. Use sparingly.*

I follow the instructions and pat the damp cloth over my sides, arms, face, and every part of my body where I feel the slightest amount of pain. Immediately, I feel the pain start to numb. A cool sensation, like a rush of water, washes over me. It's so relaxing and calming that I'm tempted to lie on the ground and soak it in, but I know I don't have time for that.

I stare at the cloth and the remaining liquid.

I look at the clock. It's 4:30 p.m.

"*It's time to get out of here,*" I think.

I place the rest of the liquid and the cloth into a bag. Then I grab a few extra knives, putting three into my bag and the last one into my pocket.

I put on the white security uniform. To my surprise, it's breathable and lightweight. It actually feels comfortable, and it fits perfectly. I note the parts of the suit that aren't shielded and could leave me open to injury.

I glance around the room, realizing this might be the last time I see it. Then I head into the hallway, walking with stern focus and determination.

At every corner, security force agents stand guard. I head toward the elevator leading to the control room, hoping to meet Alex and Titan there. I hesitate at the elevator door, trying to remember the code.

"3-3-4-2-7-8-2," I type it in. I want to breathe a sigh of relief as the door opens, but I try to stay cool. I step inside, and the doors close in front of me.

Suddenly, my messenger starts buzzing again. My heart pounds as I open it.

"**BLAKE LEVI HAS BEEN COMPROMISED. TITAN JOHNSON HAN HAS BEEN COMPROMISED. JESSIE BEAN HAS BEEN COMPROMISED. OLIVIA RONALDO HAS BEEN COMPROMISED.**" The messages flash red.

"**IMMEDIATELY HEAD FOR AN EMERGENCY EXIT! WE REPEAT, IMMEDIATELY HEAD FOR AN EMERGENCY EXIT!**"

My mind races.

"*There's no more time,*" I realize. "*There's no more plan.*"

I hit the button for the 30th floor, and the elevator shoots up. My body jolts.

"**Going to the 30th floor,**" I type in the messenger.

My body jolts again when I hear distant gunshots. I peer through the glass of the elevator toward the world below. Fighting has broken out. I send a silent prayer that Titan or Alex isn't involved.

I look back up. My heart is racing.

"*I'm prepared to die,*" I think. "*This battle is to the death.*"

I close my eyes and remember Zenya, the man tending my uncle's grave. I think of my uncle, my family, James's rebellious flowers, his mother and brother, Ray, and all the people in my faction watching from their windows at the graveyard.

Not too long ago, I was completely alone. Now, all these people are with me, depending on me. When did so many people become part of my life? I need to keep my promises to them. They've given me their trust, hope, and so much more.

The elevator doors open, and I shove a knife into the control pad. Sparks fly, and the elevator flashes red to indicate it's malfunctioning and won't move.

"*This should buy me some time,*" I think.

I turn to see a guard in a white suit staring at me in confusion. I whip out another knife and stab him in the neck. His blood squirts onto my white suit, staining it. He falls lifeless to the ground.

I hesitate for a second, wondering if I could have stopped him another way. The sound of footsteps pulls me from my thoughts. I drag his body to the corner, out of plain sight, and crouch next to it.

A man in a white lab coat with a clipboard stops in front of the giant metal doors leading to the hallway. I recognize him—my tormentor from before.

He taps a code into the door. "5-7-4-8-3-3-6."
A small metal piece slides out of the door, and a black screen with green light appears above it.

The man places his chin on the metal piece. Green lights scan his eyes, and the doors open.

I decide this is as good a chance as any. I sneak up behind him and press my knife into his back.

"Don't run. Don't scream. Don't look at me. Just keep walking, or I'll kill you," I whisper.

Shaking, the man walks forward.

"Whatever you want, you won't get it. This won't work," he says between clenched teeth.

"Take me to where the prisoners you captured last night are being held," I reply, "and shut the fuck up."

As we pass the circular hallway with the dark figures behind the glass, I try to look casual, as if I'm guarding the man in the lab coat. We reach another set of doors. He pulls out his badge and presses it against the keypad. The doors open, revealing prisoners in their cells. They are strapped to chairs, facing the walls.

These prisoners are clearly in the same reeducation program I was in.

"Take me to the prisoners who are about to be executed, quickly," I order, my eyes darting between the cells, hoping to see someone I recognize—hoping I'll find James.

He picks up his pace and turns another corner.

"Hey, Benjamin," a voice calls from behind us.

I press my knife harder into his back.

"Don't stop, but respond," I whisper.

"Uh-h... Uh-h. No, no time to chat. I'm b-busy," the man—Benjamin—stammers.

"Okay," the other man replies, his tone laced with confusion and slight suspicion.

Benjamin stops at a door in the middle of the hallway. He presses his badge into a keypad on the door. I hear a clicking sound, then he turns the knob. My eyes take a moment to adjust to the dark descending staircase in front of us. I nudge him forward, and we begin our descent.

At the bottom of the staircase, we encounter another door. He types in a code, but an error message pops up.

"What's going on?" I ask, my voice sharp.

"I-I can't remember the code," Benjamin stammers, sweat dripping from his forehead.

"If you mess up again, I will kill you," I say flatly.

Benjamin steadies himself, then types another code: "4-4-6-8-2-3-5." I hear the clicking sound of the door unlocking, and we both exhale a sigh of relief.

As soon as the door opens, the smell hits me—body odor, old blood, and other unrecognizable stenches. I gag. Benjamin seems taken aback by the scent but shrugs it off and continues walking. I follow closely behind.

In the corners of the room, I see weapons that look like something out of the Middle Ages—ropes, a finger guillotine, belts with small spikes. My stomach turns, and I fight the urge to vomit. But when I see what looks like old human skin on one of the wooden pieces, I can't hold it back. I open my helmet, allowing the full force of the stench to hit me, and vomit into a corner.

Benjamin stops and glances at me. I can see him contemplating running.

"Don't even think about it," I warn.

"Who's down there?" a woman's voice calls out.

I motion for Benjamin to respond.

"It's just me, Benjamin," he says.

"Benjamin?" The voice sounds puzzled. "What are you doing down here?"

Footsteps draw closer. I look around, but there's nowhere to hide.

"I'm giving a new employee a tour," Benjamin says, his voice trembling.

Relief washes over me at his response.

"Benjamin, you know we don't traditionally do tours down here," says the woman, rounding the corner. It's Kathryn Richards, her eyes narrowing in suspicion.

"Ms. Richards... I'm sorry," Benjamin mumbles, bowing his head.

In that instant, I see the realization dawn in Kathryn's eyes. Before I can react, she pulls out her gun and fires multiple shots in my direction. I jump, using Benjamin's body as a shield. Bullets tear through his arms, legs, and head.

I continue holding his body as I charge toward Richards. When her body collides with Benjamin's lifeless one, her gun skids across the floor. His body falls with a lifeless thud, but not before I slip his badge into my pocket.

"Help!" Richards screams. "We have an intruder! HELP!"

All chaos breaks loose. Alarms blare, and I stab her twice in the leg, leaving her on the ground, bleeding.

"*I need her alive,*" I think. "*I need to know the truth about my father.*"

Guards charge into the room. I whip out my gun and lift Richards, using her as a human shield. I shoot at the guards in succession as they attempt to enter.

I hear cheering behind me. I run down the hallway, following the voices.

"James!" I scream. "James, where are you?"

I scan the cells, seeing burnt bodies, disfigured faces, and missing limbs. Horror washes over me.

"*How could they?*" I think. "*This is horrifying.*"

"Feonix!" a woman's voice calls out. I turn and see Blake, dressed in a white soldier uniform like mine.

"They got me this morning," she says, pointing toward a small room. "Over there! He has the keychain and codes for the cells. Hurry! In minutes, this place will be overrun with soldiers, and there will be no escape."

I lock eyes with the guard in the booth. He looks terrified. I charge toward the room and lift my gun, aiming at the glass.

"Bang! Bang! Bang!" Three shots ring out, but the glass remains unscratched.

"It must be bulletproof!" Blake yells from her cell.

"The keypad!" shouts a man from another cell. "It's the only way in and out. It also has an eye scanner."

My mind races. I remember Benjamin's body and drag it toward the booth. The man inside looks even more terrified and draws his gun.

"*I'm running out of time,*" I think.

I press Benjamin's ID against the keypad. A black screen with green lights appears. I hold his eyelids open so the scanner can read his eyes. While it's scanning, I glance up and make eye contact with the guard in the booth. His hands shake as he points his gun at the door.

"Look!" I yell. "There's no reason for me to kill you if you help me!"

The latch unlocks. I release Benjamin's body, letting it fall to the ground with a thud. The man's hands tremble even more. I put my hand on the doorknob.

"Put down the gun, and I won't kill you. I promise," I say, staring him directly in the eyes.

He hesitates, then shakily lowers his gun. I open the door and kick the weapon away. The small room resembles a control center with buttons everywhere.

"Which one opens the cells?" I ask, frantically pressing as many as I can.

"I-I don't remember," he stammers.

I point my gun at his head. "Think."

His eyes dart around as he shakes his head. "B-but these are very dangerous criminals," he stammers again.

I smack him across the face with my gun. He crumples but quickly straightens, a strange resolve in his eyes.

"I told you to—" I start, but then I notice the look in his eyes isn't resolve. It's warning.

I duck just as someone fires a gun from behind me. The bullet pierces the man's head.

"He should've never let you in," the voice says.

I rip off his ID and fire multiple shots at the figures aiming at me. The prisoners rattle their cages, screaming for freedom. I shoot at the glass surrounding a giant red button that reads *DO NOT*

TOUCH. The glass shatters, and I slam my hand down on the button.

"You idiot!" one of the figures yells.

Red lights flood the room, and a timer counting down from five minutes appears on the ceiling.

"Feonix!" Blake yells from her cell. "In your bottom left pocket, there's a distress flare! They won't be able to see through it, but your helmet will let you see perfectly."

I feel around my body and pull out a small red tube. I shake it, pop the top off, and roll it into the hallway. Pink smoke quickly fills the room.

Blake's right—I can see everything. I fire shots toward my assailants, taking cover behind the control panel. With Benjamin's badge still in hand, I begin opening as many cells as I can. My heart races as part of me wonders if some of the people I'm releasing might also be a threat. But I know that right now, we share a common enemy.

"James!" I scream. "James, where are you?"

I reach Blake's cell and release her. She grabs a gun from a fallen guard and turns to cover my back.

"I think they took James somewhere else," she says. "Can we stop by another section? My sister might be there."

I glance at the timer—three minutes and thirty-seven seconds left.

"We've got to be quick," I reply while continuing to unlock cells.

The room descends into chaos. Freed prisoners run in all directions, some fighting guards while others limp toward the exits. Guns fire around us. Blake and I sprint deeper into the hallway and turn a corner, finding more cells. Hands reach through the bars, desperate for freedom.

"Please! Help me!" screams echo around us.

I unlock as many cells as I can.

"James!" I call out again, praying for a response.

"Feonix!"

My heart stops at the familiar voice. I turn and see Emre in one of the cells. Half of his face is burned, his hair missing in patches. His gray eyes lock onto mine—one of them red and swollen. Two of his fingers are gone. My breath catches as I take in the damage.

"I'm sorry," he says, his voice hoarse.

I shake my head. I can't trust him, but there's no time to wrestle with forgiveness. Without a word, I press Benjamin's ID against the keypad. The lock clicks open, and the cell door swings wide. Fear grips me for a moment, thinking he might attack, but Emre sprints toward the exit without a second glance.

"Thank you," he calls back.

"Feonix! I found her!" Blake yells. "My sister! Hurry!"

I rush toward her voice and find a brown-haired girl sitting in a cell. She looks up at me expectantly. I press the badge against the keypad, releasing her.

I check the timer—two minutes and three seconds left. Blake looks up too.

"We're out of time! We have to get out of here!" she shouts.

I run, opening more cells as fast as I can. Prisoners pour out, pushing past each other, their screams filling the air.

"James!" I shout again, just in case.

"Is Titan down here?" I ask Blake.

"I don't think so," she replies. "I think he's hiding in the building somewhere, but I'm not sure."

"Titan! Are you down here?" I call as I continue unlocking cells.

"We have to go," Blake urges.

I glance at the timer—one minute and thirteen seconds. My eyes scan the remaining cages. People scream for help, their hands reaching toward me. I know I'm out of time. My stomach clenches as I toss the ID badge toward one of the outstretched hands and sprint after Blake and her sister.

The stairwell becomes a chaotic crush of bodies. People climb over each other, desperate to escape.

"I have the key! I have the key!" I yell, but panic drowns out my voice.

"Out of the way!" Blake draws her gun and fires two shots into the ceiling. "Move, or I'll shoot you! We have the key!"

The crowd parts just enough for us to squeeze through. Blake leads the way, and I follow, clutching the other badge key. I press it against the keypad, unlocking the door. The lock clicks, and I push it open. People surge past me into the hallway. I sprint toward the exit.

A loud beep echoes behind me. I know I shouldn't turn around, but curiosity pulls at me. Flames burst into the hallway, consuming everything in their path.

My heart nearly stops. I don't even have time to feel fear. Heat licks at my back, and suddenly I'm airborne. My body slams into a wall, then another, before crashing to the floor. The whole world black.

17

Speak of the Devil

I hear a voice, low and menacing.

"You've really made a mess of things," it says. I recognize the voice as Revel's, and my heart sinks. I know I'm in trouble.

"I should have known better. I should have killed you," she continues.

As I try to move, I realize my hands and feet are bound. Panic sets in, and I start to thrash about.

"What's going on?" I demand, struggling to break free. But the bonds hold fast.

"You're a fool," Revel's voice continues. "A naive idealist, just like your father." She sighs heavily.

"What do you know about my father?" I demand, but Revel just laughs.

I strain to see her, but my eyes can't seem to focus. I notice I'm in a room I've never seen before. The room is immaculate. There's a golden chandelier on the ceiling. The chairs are made of mahogany wood, which contrasts nicely with the green houseplants in every corner. One wall has an aquarium built in with fish I'm sure are extinct in the outside world. Another wall is covered in what looks like letters—hundreds of letters from Station 7 listeners.

"I built all of this for you, Feonix," Revel continues, a bit of regret in her tone. "For you and people like you. I wanted to give you a better life, a life without fear or oppression. But your father had other ideas. He wanted to keep things the way they were, to hold onto his power and control."

I finally see Revel. She is standing in the corner. She has a cane. I've never seen her need a cane before. She must be getting worse.

"I loved you, and I loved your father. When we built Station 7 together, I believed we could take over the world! He made me feel like I could do anything," she sighs.

Revel's voice grows colder, more detached.

"Your father had to go, Feonix. He was planning something that would have destroyed everything we built."

I struggle against my bonds, but I can't seem to break free. My eyes dart from one side of the room to the other, trying to make sense of where I am and my possibility of escape.

As Revel steps closer, I see the glint of a pistol in her hand. Fear grips me. My heart feels like it will pound out of my chest. But as I begin to make sense of Revel's words, anger takes over my fear, and I refuse to give up.

"You're not going to kill me," I say, my voice shaking with rage.

"We built a vision, and then we built a family," her voice begins to shake. She leans close to my face, puts the back of her hand against my cheek, and whispers in my ear, "We... built you."

Her words send me into shock, and though she keeps talking, I don't really hear anything else she says.

"But alas, we had two different visions, and he left me," her voice stammers. "And betrayed me."

"When he returned to his wife—the woman you know as your mother—to my surprise, she took him back and took you in like her own," Revel continues. "Part of me thought it was weakness. The other part of me admired her. Even envied her."

"She could live as a mother and a wife to a man and child I loved. But I had an obligation to the world that was more than anything I ever wanted for myself," her voice is calm and sober now.

"You see, I am more than a soldier in this war. I am a general. My goal has been and continues to be to bring accountability to the powerful but also offer hope and a better future to those in need. The factions won't do it. The government won't do it. So I have to do it!"

"Station 7 has been and continues to be a beacon of light to those who need hope."

I struggle to make sense of all the things she is telling me.

"Are you insinuating that you are my mother?" I ask, hardly believing the question I just posed.

"Feonix, everything about this moment is real. I am your mother, and I will soon have to kill you."

I struggle in my chains. I want to run, scream, and call her a liar.

"I know my family, you fraud! They died years ago," I say.

"I know, in the fire. I had them killed," she says. "It wasn't easy."

A tear falls down her face.

"You know I haven't cried in years, but every time I remember losing your father, I still feel it. But do you ever wonder why you survived?" she asks. "I saved you myself."

"Liar!" I yell. "Get me out of this chair and face me, you coward!"

"I'm sorry. I know it's a lot to digest. But your father, like you, had horrible plans that would have broken public trust in the station. He couldn't see the bigger goal. And to be honest, I think he didn't want us growing without him. There was a little jealousy there," she says.

"And your sister Katheryn really proved herself. She knew the plan and followed everything through without a hitch. Even though I didn't tell her then, that was when I knew she would be my successor," she says.

"She knew her father was a traitor and had to go for the greater good of the station. Most of the plan she drew up herself. I just approved it," says Revel.

Revel's eyes pang with agony, her voice cold and calculating. Then she steps back and points the pistol in my direction.

"I'm sorry," she says. She pulls the trigger.

The next moment is less than a second but feels like forever.

The shock I feel because of her words overwhelms the threat of my imminent death. I realize I've finally discovered my truth. At the same time, my body tenses at the sound of the pop of the gun, bracing for impact.

Then I have the moment—the one all the people near death talk about. The moment where your life flashes before your eyes in an instant. Except for me, it's not my whole life, just different moments.

I don't want to believe what I'm hearing, but part of me knows it's all true. The pieces fit together like a puzzle that never made sense before. Of course, Revel is my mother, and Richards is my sister. Of course, my father and Revel were lovers. And my mother tolerated the multiple affairs. My father was brilliant and that brought him many admirers.

I think back and remember things buried in my thoughts that I never fully made sense of before—my mother, or the woman who raised me, crying in the middle of the night when my father wasn't home. Their fights. My father always operating in secret with multiple phones we were forbidden to touch.

My mother's distance from me. I spent my entire life wondering why I never felt a mother's love from the woman who raised me. Better yet, she may have known who my mother really was and resented her. Resented me. These were parts of growing up I tried to forget. But here I am, reliving it all in my mind with more clarity than ever before.

Suddenly everything goes black. I hear gunshots ring throughout the room. My entire body tenses as I brace for a bullet to hit me. But instead, I feel my body swing through the air and hit the ground. Pain throbs through my head, but somehow, I think I'm still alive. Then I hear what sounds like power shutting off. The chains on my hands, legs, and around my head loosen. They must be powered by the same energy source that just went out.

"Generators!" screams Revel. "Get them on now!"

But it's too late. I break free of my chains. When my eyes adjust, I see Revel trying to escape through the back door of her office. I immediately try to run after her, but my pace is slower due to the burns all over my body. Agony washes over me as I push forward.

"Feonix! Feonix, are you in here?"

I want to jump for joy when I hear Alex's voice.

"Alex! I'm here!" I yell back.

She runs toward me and hugs me tightly.

"I'm so relieved you're alive. A lot of people didn't make it out of that blast. You're hurt," she says, pulling her hand, stained with blood, away from my body.

She pulls out a liquid container and a napkin from her pocket—the same numbing serum I took earlier. She pours the liquid on the napkin and presses it against my left rib cage.

"You kind of need this everywhere, but we don't have much time. Titan said he could kill the power for only five minutes. This place is going to be surrounded," she says.

"Did you find James?" I ask.

"I did, but I couldn't get to him," she sighs. "He's in the projection room, where Revel does all her live shows. He's strapped down. I think she plans to make an example of him. If you're ready to go through with your plan, Titan is ready to rewire the projection room so everything goes live."

"Alex! Feonix! Are you in here?" Blake's voice calls out.

"We're here!" I yell back.

Blake and her sister step into the room.

"We need to get out of here now! Security guards are ready to storm this place!" she says.

"You're too late," another voice growls.

We all start to run. I hear gunshots, and someone screams. None of us can see clearly where we're going, but Alex holds my hand, leading me through a different door. Blake and her sister follow close behind.

The lights cut back on, and I see we're in some sort of closet. The sound of security forces stomping around the area is loud and clear. Alex points to a ventilation system, quietly opens it, and beckons for us to follow her inside.

Blake's sister goes in after Alex. Then I motion for Blake to move, but I can see from the look on her face that she's hurt. I lift her hand and see that she's been holding her side, blood gushing out of it. She's been shot.

"Go," she whispers. "Take care of my sister. I can't make it."

Tears stream down her face. I glance around, searching for anything to slow the bleeding. Blake's little sister looks at me, confused, motioning for us to hurry. I tie a blue cloth I find in the corner around Blake's wound, trying to stop the blood flow. I lift her up and push her ahead of me.

Blake's sister's face turns pale when she sees her. Tears fall down her cheeks. She drags while I push Blake through the ventilation system. We move as quietly as possible. Sweat trickles down my face. I hear soldiers running back and forth, searching for us.

Alex seems to know where she's going. Thank goodness she worked in the control center—this place feels like a maze. I keep thinking back to the maps I studied, but my brain is hazy.

Suddenly, Alex stops. She points below herself. We all remain silent except for Blake's heavy breathing.

"I'm really tired of all these ridiculous antics from you and your friends," Revel's voice echoes below. "I will show the world the traitor you really are. Betraying your own country and working for the Chinese. You almost had us fooled."

"This is ridiculous," says James.

My heart skips a beat at the sound of his voice. I want to laugh and cry, knowing he's alive.

"This is one of the lowest things I'd expect from you," he continues.

I peer through the ventilation system, trying to see below. The room looks like the inside of a news studio. There are about ten giant lights lined along the ceiling, pointing toward the center of the studio. The center has an elevated circular stage with red and white lights lining its edge. A crescent-shaped desk made of red and white glass sits atop the stage.

James is chained to a chair in front of the desk, at the center of the stage. Revel sits to his right. Another smaller table is positioned next to her.

In front of the desk, about eight feet away, are two large black cameras, both pointed toward the center stage. The back walls have wide screens that can display green backgrounds, other channels, or various imagery. Behind the cameras stands a sea of guards. I also notice guards stationed between the lights, their guns aimed at the stage.

I think to myself, *How do I get to James?*

I see Alex type a message, probably to Titan. Then she looks at us and gives a thumbs-up. Blake is pale and breathing heavily.

"We're running out of time to save her," I whisper in despair.

"You tried to take over the station so that you could begin to emit Chinese propaganda to our country's citizens. You're a spy! We've gone through all your things and seen you for who you really are. The evidence is all here," says Revel. "Richards, please get the documents."

Richards opens a bag and pulls out documents, videotapes, and other items in plastic bags. She places them on the table for everyone to see.

"In sixty seconds, the world will see who you really are and watch you pay for your crimes. Our trial has commenced, and you are guilty," says Revel.

"This is the biggest load of bullshit. I thought you were an evil mastermind. Now I see you're just evil. People will see through this," James shakes his head in disgust.

"Thirty seconds!" yells a man from behind the camera.

A man walks over and stuffs a cloth into James' mouth, using another cloth to cover it.

"I think we have to split up. One of us needs to cause a distraction," says Alex.

My mind races.

"I'll... go down into the guards and detonate," says Blake.

"Blake, no!" says her sister, desperation in her voice.

"Jessica. I love you. You know that and don't ever forget it. I wish I could be with you. I really don't want to leave you alone," tears flow down Blake's face again. "I'm not going to make it. Let me die knowing I helped save others, but most importantly, you."

Jessica begins to cry. They hug for a much shorter time than it feels in the moment.

"And we are live," says the man behind the camera.

Alex and I move to opposite sides of the studio. Jessica and Blake head toward the back of the room, where most of the guards stand. It seems like all the guns in the room are locked and loaded.

"Ladies, gentlemen, and everything in between, welcome to Station 7 tonight," Revel announces. "Each night, we work hard to uncover a story that is both shocking and shifts the world for the greater good. And tonight is no different."

"As many of you know, the competition for my replacement is one of the most coveted victories on this side of the planet. And though the details of the competition remain a sworn secret, I assure you all we do everything in our power to ensure that the competition is fair and just," Revel continues.

"Unfortunately, sometimes our best isn't good enough. Snakes with dubious intentions make their way through our ranks. This time, they made it all the way to the top," she says.

"This should be both troubling and terrifying to many of you as you know Station 7 serves as a beacon of light and hope to those who still believe in democratic society, the Fourth Estate, and holding the rich and powerful accountable. We love truth, and we die for truth," Revel declares.

"Then die now, you lying bitch!" Blake yells as she drops from the ceiling into the crowd of guards.

She pulls out the detonator and holds it above her head. With her other hand, she makes the sign of the cross as a prayer. The guards turn and immediately start shooting in her direction. Blake's body is riddled with bullets, but as soon as one makes contact with the detonator, a small explosion goes off.

Alex jumps from the ceiling, a rope in one hand and a gun in the other. She shoots down the guards stationed between the lights. From above, Jessica continues firing, running to different corners to avoid detection.

"We seem to have a little disturbance," Revel says calmly. "We will be back after a short intermission."

She runs off the stage with Richards covering her.

I sprint to James on the stage, shooting multiple guards on my way. As soon as I reach him, I try to free his arms and legs to no avail. I remove the cloth and gag from his mouth and, against my own logic, kiss his lips. I look into his eyes.

"I thought I wouldn't see you alive again. How do I get these chains off you?"

"I love you. But you need to get out of here—you could get shot. Richards is the only one with the key," says James.

"They won't shoot you if the cameras are on you!" Alex yells. "Go live now!"

I look up and see Alex sticking her gun in the back of the cameraman. The room is smoky, with injured and bleeding guards lying all around. I shoot at two guards aiming at Alex.

"And we are live," the cameraman announces.

I look into the camera. I've practiced this speech a million times, but it's only at this moment I realize I never truly believed our plan would work. I search my mind for the right words.

"Good evening, everyone. My name is Feonix Cheenoma, daughter of the late Fred Cheenoma and Victoria Revel," I pause, taking in everything I just said.

"For the last five years, I've worked as an editor at Station 7. Like many others, I joined the competition to take over. But recently, I learned that everything I've worked for and the history of my entire life has been a lie—an elaborate lie designed and executed by our beloved Station 7 hero, who I recently came to know as my mother, Victoria Revel," I continue.

"There is no competition. Revel already knows who she wants to take over the station. But more importantly, the pure truths Station 7 has been known for have been corrupted. The stories you see are laced with half-truths and—"

"Liar!" Revel storms back onto the stage, her cane tapping loudly with each step. "You are a liar and an opportunist, trying to take over the station! You are a fraud! She posed as an editor, then led a rebellion within the station to try to take it over by force!"

I look at Revel, then back at the cameras.

"Soon, you will see stories from the past, but stories only done in part. However, this time, you will see full accountability—not just for those who are against Revel or the station," I declare.

"Do not let yourselves be deceived by these lies," says Revel. "I have and will always put the truth forth in our work!"

"Well, is this the truth?" I ask.

Behind me, images from the reeducation center and torture chambers flash on the wide screens.

"That Station 7 hosts brainwashing stations and torture chambers within its walls?" I ask. "Is it true that those who believe in truly doing the job of news—without biased idealistic reform—are tortured?"

"This..." Revel pauses, laughs, and begins to clap. "What a show. You have to be kidding. Anyone watching this knows that this is all fake—made up so a poor girl who lost the competition could attempt to take over by force."

"And now the show is over. Get off the stage," says Richards, stepping out with her gun drawn and aimed directly at me.

"What are you going to do? Kill me on live television?" I ask.

"Yes, because I have to protect Station 7 from dangerous people like you. The world relies on this," Richards says.

"And the world has been deceived," I reply.

I feel the weight of a tug-of-war for popular opinion. Seeing Richards and knowing what she did to my family makes my blood boil, but I try to choose my words and movements with care. I can tell Richards is doing the same. It's like we are in the middle of a presidential debate—except there's no moderator to fact-check, and if I lose, I will be shot.

"This is what you've been doing! Killing and torturing people based on your own system. Democratic societies like the one you claim to uphold have a justice system, and this isn't it," I say sternly. "There's a right thing to do, Katheryn. You can atone for the death, the killings, and everything else if you come clean now."

"We all know our current justice system is broken—favoring the rich and the powerful more than it ever has in the past. We dreamed of helping to restore democracy and free society," Richards says, moving her finger toward the trigger. "But we are far from where we need to be."

My mind races. I could reach for my gun, but she would immediately shoot James and me. I think hard about what to say, but no more good words come to mind. I'm stuck.

"*I'm going to die,*" I think. "*I can only hope that all of this is worth it.*"

My mind flashes through images—my family, my little sister with her beautiful smile, making love to James, sleeping in his arms, and the beautiful drawing of Istanbul he made for me. I think of Ray and Titan, how friendly they always were together. I think of Blake and the bullet holes in her body. I think of how brave she was as she died, raising the grenade above her head. I think of Gabby. I think of my father and my uncle. I whisper my gratitude to him for getting me this far. Then, I brace myself.

"Also," says Richards after a pause, "there's no atonement for a woman like me."

And with that, it feels like the world suddenly moves in slow motion. Richards shifts her gun, aims, and pulls the trigger. The bullet flies through the air. James' eyes widen as they follow the bullet. I open mine wide, waiting for the impact. Alex shuts her eyes as if the bullet is coming for her. The cameraman's mouth gapes open. The remaining guards tilt their heads slightly, following the bullet. Revel's confident, stern expression shifts to one of terror as the bullet strikes her right between the eyes.

The room is silent as Revel falls to the ground. The sound is lighter than you'd imagine—a soft thump—reflecting how much weight she lost through her sickness. Then the room erupts in chaos.

Bullets fly across the room toward the stage. I knock James to the ground, still strapped to the chair. I scream as a bullet hits my arm. Alex lies on the ground, shot multiple times but still moving. The cameraman is dead. Richards is on the ground. I can't tell if she's alive or dead.

Suddenly, Jessica starts firing from above. She jumps down and continues shooting until all the guards in the room are dead.

The room is a bloody mess. I rip off a piece of my shirt and tie it around my arm to stop the bleeding. Jessica runs to Alex, and so do I. I take the rest of my shirt and press it against Alex's wounds.

"Get her to the infirmary, quickly. There isn't much time," I say to Jessica.

She nods, lifts Alex's body, and carries her out of the room.

I walk up to Richards.

"Are you still going to try to kill me?" I ask.

"Would I kill my own sister?" Richards chuckles weakly.

"Well," I say, unsure how to respond.

"Where's your sense of humor?" says Richards. "My whole life, I've been like a dog to her. I did everything she asked, thinking I was doing the right thing. Thinking I was making my mother proud. I'm not proud of all I've done."

Richards pauses and coughs. Blood leaks from her lips.

"Dad knew her plans for the station were deviating from the original mission, and he wanted to oust her as the leader," says Richards. "Mom said the only way he would stop was if he was dead, so she asked me to come up with a plan. That night, I thought he was the only one in the home. I didn't want to kill the whole family. Things got out of hand. But I think she knew. I'm sorry. Since then, I've never seen myself as anything but a cold-blooded murderer."

I just stare at her. I don't know what to make of her words. Am I supposed to feel sorry for her? I don't know what to feel or think. She winces and coughs again, more blood pouring from her mouth. I can tell she doesn't have much time.

"The world should know. Station 7 is a beautiful thing in an ugly world. And it is so important who takes over this station—someone who will lead it with truth and integrity. This is the hope of our nation. The restoration of a free society. Mom and I tainted that, but if you take over, I believe that can change. There's no atonement for a woman like me, but this is the closest I can get to it," Richards says.

She coughs again, barely breathing now.

"Here," she says, handing me an ID badge and a key. "These should get you access to all you need."

I take the keys and ID, still in shock. I suddenly remember James is still strapped in the corner. I turn around and see the camera is still on. I walk up to it and turn it off.

Then I rush to James. He's still lying on the ground, stuck in the position I left him in. I use the key from Richards to set him free. He hugs me tightly. I wince from the pain.

"Oh, sorry! We need to get this looked at now," he says.

"I'm alright," I protest. "We're alive."

He smiles at me.

18

The Price of Leadership

The months that follow are like a blur. I take over as interim leader of Station 7 until I am officially voted in by the newly formed, democratically selected board.

I also purge the Station of Rivers' spies and Revel loyalists. Many sign agreements that we draft to let them leave with a generous severance package. I know some still remain, but I try not to let myself become paranoid about it.

I appoint Titan as the Director of Content Strategy and Innovation at the Station, and Jessica as the head of all personnel. James takes a top post as the lead producer and editor. Alex remains in a coma for months, and we agree to allow her to live as long as she is willing to fight to survive.

Outside the Station, things are chaotic. The stories we release cause a whirlwind of killings, fights, debates, and lasting distrust in faction leaders and Station 7. Many people turn to anarchy, fearing they don't know who to trust.

The Station's reserves decline steadily as donations dry up and listenership depletes. Each month, I look at the notes and reports and despair. I make tours to different factions, introducing myself and trying to educate them about the new Mission. I also try to answer questions about the old failings of the Station, but none of it seems to work. At some faction visits, people seem to adore me. At others, they try to kill me.

James, who lives with me now, tries to assure me that in a few years, if we hang on, things will turn around. He tells me people are still in shock and will be for a long time. I don't know how he can be so sure. My days waver between complete despair and gratitude for the life James and I have been given together.

Then one day, my phone rings. Since I am reviewing reports, I refuse to pick it up. Jessica enters my office.

"There's a call for you. I think you should take it," she says sheepishly.

"Who is it?" I finally look up from my desk.

"President Rivers," she says, then exits the room.

I stare at the call on hold on my office phone. I've never spoken to President Rivers. I wonder what she knows about me, but I know, for the most part, I don't trust her. I think about the chaos in the streets and realize the current situation must be bad for the government—or what's left of it. Then I pick up the phone and press the red button, releasing Rivers from hold.

"Hello?" I say.

I hear the sound of hands clapping.

"Hello?" I repeat, more sternly this time.

"Wow, Feonix!" President Rivers' voice sounds excited but still a bit raspy. "That was quite the show. I don't think I could have done a better job no matter how hard I tried."

"What exactly do you want?" I ask, finding myself annoyed but also deeply curious.

"Look, I heard the Station has been struggling. And I want to let you know that I believe in the fourth estate, as the vision you have set forth," says Rivers. "I think you and I can start over. I have a proposition for you."

A Note from the Author

Thank you for reading Book 1 of The Herd Series, *The Herd-When Democracy Falls*! I hope you enjoyed it as much as I loved writing it.

If you have a moment, I'd truly appreciate it if you could leave a review on Amazon, Goodreads, or your favorite book platform. Reviews help other readers discover the book and allow me to keep writing stories like this one. Your support means the world!

Want to stay in the loop about my next book? *The sequel is coming soon!* Be the first to get updates, exclusive sneak peeks, and special content by signing up for my mailing list at **www.jennyabamu.com**.

You can also connect with me on:
📖 Goodreads: https://tinyurl.com/5d4xk732
📱 Instagram: @jenny.abamu
🔗 LinkedIn: https://www.linkedin.com/in/jennyabamu/
✉️ Newsletter: **www.jennyabamu.com**

Thank you for being part of this journey. Until next time!

www.ingramcontent.com/pod-product-compliance
Lightning Source LLC
Chambersburg PA
CBHW050019120726
47903CB00006B/1832